PUFFIN BOOKS

THE MAJORLY AWKWARD BFF DRAMAS OF LOTTIE BROOKS

KATIE KIRBY

PUFFIN

PUFFIN BOOKS

UK | USA | Canada | Ireland | Australia
India | New Zealand | South Africa

Puffin Books is part of the Penguin Random House group of companies
whose addresses can be found at global.penguinrandomhouse.com.

www.penguin.co.uk   www.puffin.co.uk   www.ladybird.co.uk

First published 2024
001

Text design by Kim Musselle
Printed and bound in Great Britain by Clays Ltd, Elcograf S.p.A.

The authorized representative in the EEA is Penguin Random House Ireland,
Morrison Chambers, 32 Nassau Street, Dublin D02 YH68

A CIP catalogue record for this book is available from the British Library

HARDBACK
ISBN: 978–0–241–64725–7

TRADE PAPERBACK
ISBN: 978–0–241–67688–2

EXPORT PAPERBACK
ISBN: 978–0–241–64740–0

All correspondence to:
Puffin Books
Penguin Random House Children's
One Embassy Gardens, 8 Viaduct Gardens, London SW11 7BW

For three of my favourite fans –
Kobe, Serena and Nina x

NEW YEAR'S DAY

9.04 a.m.

Me

New year, new diary, new multipack of KitKat Chunkys and a new BOYFRIEND!!!! Could life get **ANY** better?!?!?!

I'm so blissfully happy right now that when Toby farted in my left nostril, I could barely even smell it. And when Bella ate my favourite tinted lip balm and stuck her fingers into my favourite bronzer, I . . . well, TBH that was actually pretty annoying . . . but I slammed my bedroom door shut much more gently than I usually would have! At the end of a day, it's just a tinted lip balm and bronzer, and I'm not the one who is angrily trying to get the stains out of the carpet with Vanish, am I?

Who cares about tinted lip balms and bronzers when you are in luuuurrrrrrrve?!

Not me! **NOOOOOO** siree!

I just know that this year is going to be **INCREDIBLE**. I can feel it in my eyelids.

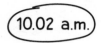

Got started on my NYD resolutions. So far I have . . .

Lottie's New Year's Resolutions

1. Try not to be quite so obsessed with KitKat Chunkys.

2. Pay someone a compliment every day!

3. Convince Mum and Dad to increase my pocket money by 50%.

4. Get eyebrow hair to grow more symmetrically.

5. Stop saying OMG (as much).

6. Get up at 7 a.m. on the weekends and do some yoga/meditation.

7. Develop my own unique sense of style.

8. Be more tolerant of my very intolerable siblings.

9. Try not to be quite so weird.

10. Meet Taylor Swift.

Number 1 is not going too well because I ate two KitKat Chunkys while writing the list, but I'm going to put the packet away now and not have another for at least two hours.

10.45 a.m.

I keep daydreaming about last night. So many high points: the dancing, the red cups, the public declaration of love (well, maybe not 'love' but 'like' or whatever) . . . and the KISS!!!

I have been filling in the hammies, in minute detail – they are utterly enthralled!

I think the kiss was the best kiss of my life. OK, I know I've only had two, but I think it was better than the first one. Not by much though . . . maybe like 15% better.

I wonder if Daniel thought it was better?

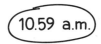

10.59 a.m.

OMG, what if Daniel thought the kiss was worse?!
What if he thought it was 15% worse than last time . . .
or 52% worse! OR 78.9% worse?!

EEEEEK! THIS SOUNDS LIKE A TRICKY MATHS QUESTION!!

Q4. If Daniel rated his first kiss with Lottie 9/10 and his
second kiss with Lottie 2.5/10, by what percentage has the
quality of Lottie's kisses decreased?

I'm not actually going to work that out because:

A. I don't want to know.

B. I'm not the kind of gal that does maths for fun.

BUT what if every time I kiss Daniel it gets worse and
worse and worse until it's 10,000 times worse? Is that
even scientifically possible?!

AHHHH! What if it's scientifically impossible to kiss

someone who is a worse kisser than me, because
I have become the WORST KISSER IN THE ENTIRE
WORLD?!

STOP.

This daydream has turned bad. Must go and do
something to end this worry spiral. Perhaps I need
some more snacks . . .

11.23 a.m.

Had some pickled-onion Monster Munch and I feel
slightly better about the kiss. Which is strange because
if I were to kiss Daniel now, it would deffo be a bad kiss
as it would taste of pickled onion.

11.26 a.m.

Although TBH I wouldn't mind a kiss that tasted
of pickled-onion Monster Munch but each to their
own.

12.05 p.m.

Mum came into my room to give me some laundry
to put away and she saw all the crisp and KitKat
wrappers and got quite cross because she is making
a roast dinner and 'I'd better eat it all or else'.

'Or else what?' I said.

'Don't be smart with me, young lady.'

'I'm not! It was a genuine question.'

'Or else . . . you'll be in trouble.'

'What kind of trouble?'

She huffed in an annoyed way and said, 'Trust me, you
don't want to know.' And then she walked out!

Happy New Year to you too, Mother!

The thing is – I did want to know though. That's why I
asked. IMO parents should be more specific with their

threats or how else are we meant to know if we should take them seriously or not?

3.44 p.m.

We had roast beef and Yorkshire puddings for our NYD lunch. The Fun Police didn't have any wine as they have decided to do Dry January – I wish they wouldn't bother as it always makes them dead miserable.

We had some crackers leftover from Christmas, so Mum had put them out too. I got a fortune-telling fish in mine and Toby got a turkey shooter, which he fired right at me and hit me on the forehead. I jumped off my chair, ready to retaliate with some mild violence, when I remembered my resolution of being more tolerant – so I took a deep breath and sat back down again.

'That was very mature, Lottie,' said Dad.

'Yes, well, trying to be kinder to my siblings was one of my New Year's resolutions.'

Toby laughed, said, 'Excellent!' and raised the turkey shooter to fire it again.

'TOBY, that's enough,' said Mum. 'Perhaps it would be a good idea if you followed in your sister's footsteps and made some resolutions too . . .'

That shut him up.

'So, you've been rather quiet about last night, Lottie Potty,' said Dad, taking a sad sip of his Ribena.

'Your dad's right – tell us all the juicy goss!' said Mum.

'Yeh, did you get all smoochy-smoochy with anybody?' Toby laughed, before puckering his lips and making awful kissing sounds.

My face, as usual, utterly betrayed me by turning a bright shade of strawberry.

'SHE DID, SHE DID!' squealed Toby, clearly delighted with himself.

'BUUUUUUMMMM!' shouted Bella.

'Well, this is exciting! Come on, Lottie,' said Mum. 'Tell us everything!'

I groaned, but I figured I was better off getting it all out in the open and dealing with this cringefest in one go.

'OK, well, Daniel may have asked me to be his girl-friend . . .'

'Ewww, gross!' said Toby.

I gave him a kick under the table (my tolerance levels were in a sharp decline).

'Toby, be kind,' warned Mum, before reaching over to give me a hug. 'That's great news, love. Isn't it, Bill?'

Dad frowned. 'Hmm, I'll have to get to know the boy better before I decide that. Let me know when he's available to come round for a *man-to-man* chat.'

I must have looked horrified because Mum slapped him on the arm and said, 'Stop teasing her!'

I sincerely hope he was joking.

6.45 p.m.

The Queens of Eight Green WhatsApp group:

> **AMBER:** Happy New Year again, everybody! Anyone made any resolutions?

> **POPPY:** Nah, my mum said I'm perfect just the way I am 😇

AMBER: All mums say that, it's just #FakeNews – no offence, Poppy, but you could possibly make a few self-improvements #JustSaying

POPPY: 🙁 Like what?

AMBER: Well, I don't want this to come across in the wrong way, but your breath smells a little like hot tuna and your voice can be slightly on the screechy side too. I'd try and bring it down a pitch or two, maybe?

JESS: Amber, don't be horrible. Poppy has a lovely voice!

AMBER: I'm not being horrible! I'm trying to help her. We've all noticed the hot tuna breath, right?

(Long pause in the convo.)

MOLLY: Umm . . . Lottie, have you made any resolutions?

AMBER: Don't get me started on Lottie. I could think of at least twenty.

ME: Well, I actually only have ten, OK – sorry we can't all be as perfect as you, Amber!

AMBER: I never said I was perfect. I'll certainly be trying to stop looking down on people less fortunate than myself.

JESS: Not sure it's going very well TBH.

ME: Mine aren't going very well either. I can't stop eating KitKat Chunkys!

MOLLY: Well, maybe start with something more achievable. What else do you have on the list?

ME: Hmmm, let's see . . . Stop being so weird/awkward . . . Become BFFs with Taylor Swift.

AMBER: She said 'achievable', Lottie!

JESS: I can't believe you'd ditch me for Tay-Tay ☹ ☹ ☹

ME: OMG, I'm gonna have to redo my list, aren't I?!

ME: OMG, I'm DEFINITELY going to have to redo my list. I just realized I am also meant to stop saying OMG so much!

POPPY: You guys crack me up 🤣

AMBER: You guys give me a headache!! 🤣

MOLLY: I've gotta go. Mum's just called me down for dinner, but shall we meet up tomorrow? I'm desperate for a NYE debrief and by that, Lottie, I'm looking at you! 👀 💋 🖤

ME: A lady does not kiss and tell . . .

AMBER: Oh, come on, Lottie! You know you're desperate to fill us in on every minute detail 😑

JESS: Well, I'm excited to hear the deets. Shall we say 12 p.m. at the churros stand?

MOLLY: Good plan. I could murder me some churros.

ME: See ya there. Oh and re the hot fishy breath, Poppy . . . I don't mind it – I mean who doesn't like a tuna melt?! It's a classic.

POPPY: Ahhh, thanks, Lotts xx

(8.22 p.m.)

My **BOYFRIEND** just called me.

'Hi, Lottie – Happy New Year.'

'Hi, Daniel – Happy New Year. I think we said that last night . . .'

'Yeh, we probably did. What you been up to?'

'Not much. I wrote some resolutions this morning, but they aren't going that well.'

'Really? How come?'

'I think I made them too hard. The first one was to stop eating so many KitKat Chunkys, and I've already had . . .' I looked around my bedroom floor, counting the number of discarded wrappers. 'Well, let's just say I kinda failed.'

Daniel laughed. 'You need to make them more achievable, Lottie.'

'So people keep telling me.'

'I've got a good one for you: *hang out with Daniel lots.*'

I grinned. 'That does sound more achievable.'

'Cool – when's good for you?'

'How about Saturday? We could go to the cinema?'

'Great, I'll look up what's showing.'

'OK, see ya, Daniel.'

'See ya, Lottie.'

Was about to go to sleep and then I remembered my fortune-teller fish. I ran down to the kitchen and found her on the dining table. I took her back up to my room and decided to name her Felicity.

I put her in the palm of my left hand and asked her what the future held for me and Daniel. Felicity's head and tail immediately began to twitch, so I looked up what that meant on the card and guess what . . .

OMG!!! she said we're IN LOVE!

I did not. I said quit screeching – I've got a headache! Also my name is Brian.

MONDAY 2 JANUARY

$\left(\text{9.52 a.m.} \right)$

I set my alarm for 6.30 a.m. for my yoga/meditation sesh, but the next thing I knew it was 9 a.m. and my alarm was smashed to pieces on the other side of the room. Putting two and two together, I can only assume I threw it across the room in a sleep-induced rage.

Man, these New Year's resolutions are **HARD**.

Honestly though – it was freezing and pitch-black. How can I expect myself to get up in the middle of the night?! It's just not possible.

Still . . . *Better late than never*, I thought, and I rolled out of bed and on to the carpet (with my duvet over me as it was chilly). I thought I'd start in child's pose, because I had landed in a ball anyway, but I must have fallen asleep again because the next thing I knew it was twenty minutes later . . .

Teenager's pose:
Like child's pose but with a
duvet and optional dribbling

I also had the worst pins and needles of my life!

I don't even really understand what the feeling of pins and needles is. I mean, it feels a bit like your legs don't exist any more and have been replaced by jelly legs, which are then being electrocuted, but it doesn't hurt exactly. It just feels strangely horrible and makes you want to shout stuff like . . .

'STOP IT, LEGS! STOP IT NOW!'

Which I obviously did do, because Dad appeared at my bedroom door, looking concerned. 'What's going on, Lottie? Are you OK?' he asked.

'Nothing, Dad. My legs are just being stupid.'

Dad laughed. 'Ahhh, yes – stupid legs. A classic ailment.'

'I got up early to do yoga,' I explained. 'I think my limbs are protesting.'

'Good for you, love! I wish I could get up early to exercise, but it's so cold and dark out there at the moment that I'd end up throwing my alarm clock at the wall, ha ha.'

'Thanks, Dad. It's errr . . . fine when you get used to it.'

OMG, how am I turning into such a good fibber?!

To atone for my laziness, I decided to try meditation instead. I started OMMMING, but I got bored after about two minutes and ended up watching an Instagram reel of a hydraulic press crushing various items – the bowling ball was my fave.

Saw Mum in the kitchen and I said, 'You look really lovely today, Mother.'

'Lottie, are you being sarcastic? Because I'm not in the mood.'

'No, of course not.'

She stared at me like I was crazy. 'I'm in my dressing gown, I've not even brushed my hair, which I think may have some baby sick in it, and I've got bags under my eyes the size of a small country thanks to your sister kindly allowing me approximately two hours of sleep last night. *Are you being sarcastic?*'

I looked at her properly and realized she was right: she did look absolutely awful, like a walking dead body or something. I tried to find something nice to say, *anything*, but it was very hard.

'Oh, right, yeh . . . well . . . your ears . . . look nice.'

'Thanks, Lottie. I've always aspired to having nice ears . . . Now what is it you want?'

'I don't want anything. I was just trying to pay you a compliment, that's all!'

GAH! These resolutions were proving impossible. I'd already failed at Numbers 1, 3, 5 and 8 and it hadn't even been twenty-four hours yet – then I remembered Number 3 . . .

'Oh, actually, Mum, there is something I do want. Can you increase my pocket money? I was thinking that an extra tenner would –'

'Umm, let's see . . . How about NO?'

JEEEEEEEZ – what's got into her?!

4 p.m.

Had a nice arvo with TQOEG.

We all had a bit of Chrimbo moola to spend so we did our usual crawl of Churchill Square. We started with

H&M, where I gave the girls a blow-by-blow account of my NYE kiss and the statistical evaluation of my kissing performance.

Amber was super rude as usual and kept yawning and interrupting the conversation to say stuff like, 'Would anyone prefer to talk about something more interesting, such as our geography homework or the impacts of globalization?'

'OOH, I've not done that yet,' said Poppy with a panicked look on her face.

'No one's done it yet, Poppy. I was being sarcastic,' huffed Amber impatiently. 'We do our homework on the last day of the holidays, remember?'

'Oh . . . right, yeh,' Poppy replied while picking up a sequin bomber jacket. 'How about this for your cinema date tomorrow, Lottie?'

I nodded and tried it on. It was super cute – if a little 'out there'.

'Ta-da!' I said, spinning round for the girls to see.

The rest of the girls seemed to like it, but Amber was unimpressed . . .

'Amber! Don't be mean – I think it looks great,' said Jess.

I smiled weakly but put the jacket back on the hanger. Amber was probably right: it wasn't really very me.

'OK,' said Molly, clapping her hands. 'Let's all work together on Operation Find Lottie a Date Outfit!'

I smiled. 'That would be great. One of my other resolutions was to develop my own sense of style.'

Amber looked me up and down and said, 'Well, it's going to be a difficult job.'

I suddenly felt quite self-conscious in my slightly stained hoodie, old jeans and battered trainers.

'Amber!' Molly chastised. 'What's got into you today?'

Poppy looked at Amber quizzically. 'Has something happened to upset you?'

'No. Nothing's happened!' replied Amber, looking impatient.

I sighed. 'Don't worry – she's only saying the truth. I just look . . . meh.'

'You look fine. We're all wearing practically the same outfit,' said Jess.

'Exactly,' replied Amber, surveying the group with disdain.

'TBH you could all do with a complete wardrobe make-over, but we don't have time for that. And, as hard as it is to believe that Lottie is the only one of us with a boyfriend, I guess we should start with her.'

I frowned. 'Thanks . . . I think.'

Jess started to protest. 'Well, I think you –'

'Be quiet, Jess. I'm trying to think.' Amber rested her chin in her hand as if in deep thought. 'I know what you need – a signature look.'

'A what??'

'A signature look – you know, like Taylor Swift's heavy fringe, or how Harry Styles dresses like a granny.'

'Well, Lottie already has one!' offered Poppy. 'High pony and a red hair bobble!'

Amber sighed. 'A red hair bobble is not a signature look, and she only wears it like that because she can't be bothered to do anything else with her hair.'

'Hey, that's not true!' I said, even though it was.

'It needs to be something cool, trendy and original. Something that screams Lottie Brooks – but in a good way,' she explained.

So that was it. I was a little unsure but I quite liked being a project for the gang, so we set to work. No one was going home until we'd nailed my signature look.

However, as it turned out, Amber quickly lost enthusiasm. When I didn't like her suggestions of always wearing heavy black eyeliner (too much hassle), a Nike bucket hat (looked silly), or various items of clothing that were SO not me, she got bored and dragged Molly and Poppy off to Space NK to look at super-expensive make-up.

So . . . finding my signature look was down to me and Jess. We went to grab a bubble tea (yes, I know Mum probably wouldn't approve!) and wandered round the shops, looking at different options.

'Massive hoop earrings?' suggested Jess.

'Hmm, I'd keep getting them caught on stuff,' I replied.

'Cherry DMs?'

'Too expensive.'

'Dye your hair purple?'

'I'm still traumatized from the home highlights and I'm not sure school would allow it.'

'Glasses?'

I frowned. 'Bit strange to suddenly start wearing glasses for no reason . . .'

'Sunglasses then?'

'In the cinema?!'

'Good point . . . Oooh, nose piercing!'

'Ouch!'

'Tattoo?'

'Ouch . . . and illegal.'

'Fake moustache?'

I laughed. 'I kinda like that but not sure it's that practical.'

Jess giggled. 'I guess if you kiss Daniel, it might get a bit tickly.'

The thought of kissing Daniel again made me feel a bit nervous, and I blushed, turning away from Jess so she didn't see.

'Ooh, I've got it!' said Jess suddenly. I looked over and she was holding something behind her back.

'What??'

'Ta-da!' she said, whipping out a pair of earmuffs. And when I say earmuffs, they weren't just any earmuffs – they were hamburger earmuffs.

I grinned, taking them off her. 'These are pretty cool . . . Not sure what Amber would think though –'

'Urgh, who cares what Amber thinks. She won't like anything we pick anyway.'

'True.'

I put them on my head and looked in the mirror. I **LOVED** them, so I bought them and immediately kept them on . . . but as predicted, when we met up with Amber and the others later on, she was NOT impressed.

'Novelty earmuffs? Seriously?' she said, shaking her head.

Poppy grinned. 'I really like them!'

Amber glared at Poppy and folded her arms. 'When I said *signature look*, I did not mean two massive Big Macs on the side of your head.'

'I think they look more like Whoppers, personally,' I

said, which made everyone laugh (everyone except Amber, obvs).

'When people talk about you, do you really want them to say, *You know Lottie, the girl with burger earmuffs?*'

I thought about it. 'Kinda – yeh.'

'Oh, for goodness' sake,' she huffed. 'Molly – are you going to back me up here?'

Molly shrugged. 'Well, you did say that the signature look should scream Lottie, and errr . . . I guess it does.'

'I don't know why I bother trying to help,' Amber said, before storming off in a strop.

'Amber didn't help anyway,' said Jess, 'She got bored and left me and Lottie to it – I mean, what did she expect would happen?'

I laughed. 'Exactly! She should be glad we didn't go with the fake moustache!'

4.46 p.m.

Went to get myself a KitKat Chunky from the snack drawer and there were none!

Yep, you read that right: NONE. Nada. Zero. Zilch.

So I went to find Mum to ask her what was going on.

'I've thrown them all in the bin,' she told me.

I nearly fainted. **'YOU'VE THROWN THEM IN THE BIN?!?!?!'**

'Yes. Along with the crisps and beige freezer food.'

OMG they're literally ALL my favourites!!

'Why? How?! Why? How?! **WHYYYYYYYYY????'**

Mum sighed and shook her head. 'Because, Lottie, they're not very good for you. I've been reading a book about ultra-processed foods (UPFs) that Auntie Emily got me for Christmas – it's really quite shocking. Did you know –'

'But that's not fair! Just because you're doing Dry January doesn't mean we all have to be miserable!'

'Hang on a minute – I thought, you said you wanted to cut down on KitKats as one of your New Year's resolutions . . .'

'I know what I said, but I say a lot of things – you should know by now not to take me seriously!'

'Well, I'm sorry, Lottie, but there will be no more until the end of January, and hopefully we'll all feel better for it.'

'I won't feel better, because I already feel tired and hungry and terrible.'

'That's because your body is craving sugar, but it's not what it really needs. If you listen to it carefully, it will tell you that it wants something filling and nutritious like –' she flicked through her book – 'like a boiled egg.'

A boiled egg? Was she having a laugh?!

'Well, I think you're wrong, so let's ask my body then, shall we?'

It didn't work. Mum said I couldn't just put on a funny voice and pretend it was my body talking. She also said – and this is the worst part – that Pot Noodles are UPFs too. I'm devastated!

6.45 p.m.

WhatsApp message from Poppy:

> **POPPY:** Hey! Good to see ya today. I'm a bit worried about Amber. Did you think she seemed OK?

ME: Hmmm. Mostly. I guess she was a little moodier than normal?

POPPY: Yeh, that's what I thought. I asked her how her Christmas holidays were going, and she just said, 'Terrible!' and changed the subject.

ME: You think something happened?

POPPY: I'm not sure. It's hard to say as she doesn't really like to talk about her feelings.

ME: I know. I hope she's OK.

POPPY: Me too. I'm sure it's nothing. Anyway, I'd best go. I've got to shave my big toe – for some reason the one on the right grows weird black hairs.

ME: What about the one on the left?

POPPY: Smooth as a baby's butt #GoFigure

ME: Love you, Pops, hairy toe and all 🤣

THOUGHT OF THE DAY:

After chatting to Poppy, I started thinking
about Amber and how she had seemed
different this afternoon. She's always a bit,
shall we say . . . honest?! But she was verging
on mean today – kinda what she used to be
when I first met her. I wonder if something
did happen over Christmas that she doesn't
want to tell us about . . .

TUESDAY 3 JANUARY

(11.05 a.m.)

Today is the last day of the Christmas holidays before we go back to school (sob sob). As I've got nothing planned, I decided to dedicate today to my eyebrows (AKA Resolution Number 4).

(11.09 a.m.)

Currently trying to will my right eyebrow to grow. It's definitely sparser than the left side. Perhaps I should try plucking some of the hairs on the left side to even them out a bit.

(11.15 a.m.)

Plucked a few too many hairs out of the left side, so that now looks sparser than the right.

(11.22 a.m.)

Plucked the right a bit more and you guessed it . . .

That's now less hairy than the left.

11.29 a.m.

Just going to do one or two more hairs . . .

11.41 a.m.

Or twelve more. I mean, who's counting?! Certainly not me.

11.50 a.m.

Should probably stop plucking. It's not working out very well for me.

11.55 a.m.

Just one more . . . and one more . . . and one more.

11.59 a.m.

CAN'T.

STOP.

PLUCKING!

(12.04 p.m.)

Messaged TQOEG.

> **ME:** SOMEBODY HELP ME. I DON'T KNOW MY OWN MIND ANY MORE. I HAVE BECOME POSSESSED BY A PAIR OF TWEEZERS!!

(12.11 p.m.)

OMG, where have my eyebrows gone?!?!??!?!?!!!!!!!!!!!!!!!!!

(12.17 p.m.)

I remember reading an article
about manifesting.
Apparently, if you visualize
something you really want, you
can make it happen.

12.20 p.m.

It does not matter how much I try – I cannot manifest my eyebrows back on to my face!!!!

12.28 p.m.

A knock on the door. It's Jess. She's screaming at me to put my hands in the air.

OMG, I'm totally bald above my eyes.

My forehead is just a great expanse of nothingness!

Everyone at school will laugh at me tomorrow and I'll get another awful nickname like 'Lottie No Eyebrows' or 'Massive Forehead Girl' or something even worse but I can't think of any clever eyebrow puns right now because I'm so stressed out.

The only good news is that Amber is also on her way round with her make-up bag to try to rectify the situation.

'OMG, I look a bit like an alien – or a worm or a thumb,' I moaned to the girls.

'I personally think you look more like a beluga whale,' said Amber.

'It's not that bad,' said Jess, clearly trying to calm me down.

'It IS that bad, Jess,' argued Amber. 'She has forehead baldness!'

'Some people might think it looks edgy . . . or fashionable . . .'

Amber rolled her eyes. 'Well, I guess it could be her new signature look,' she said sarcastically.

I put my head in my hands. 'Guys, I *know* I look stupid, OK. But will you help me . . . please?'

Amber started rifling through her make-up bag. 'I can try my best, but I'm not a miracle worker!'

I took a deep breath and crossed my fingers.

3.05 p.m.

All I can say is THANK GOODNESS for eyebrow pencils and **THANK GOODNESS** for Amber, who is an utter genius with them.

She drew my eyebrows back on and they look so
realistic that I think they look even better than they
did before. Definitely more even anyway.

I was so relieved that I gave her a big hug! I think she
didn't enjoy it very much.

6.45 p.m.

As soon as I walked into the kitchen for dinner, I was
suspicious.

'What is that?' I asked.

'Bolognese,' said Mum.

'That is not bolognese,' said Toby.

'Yes, it is. It's lentil and mushroom bolognese. You can't even tell the difference!'

Toby looked like he was going to cry. 'Why is the pasta brown?'

'It's wholewheat – nutritious *and* yummy!' said Mum.

Long story short: Toby refused to even try it, Bella threw it across the floor, I really tried to like it but ewwwww! What even are lentils?! Small circles of evil?!

Dad ate his but looked like he was trying not to gag.

I do not like Health-Kick Mum – I hope the normal version returns soon.

7.23 p.m.

Tried to have a nice relaxing bath to wind down and the Fun Police start shouting through the door, 'Have you done your homework, Lottie?!'

I was annoyed because, I mean, have they any idea what a stressful day I've had?! Also, I had completely forgotten about my homework, and they should have reminded me earlier in the day (obvs).

I got out of the bath and quickly dried myself off. I bumped into Mum on the way to my room. 'I wish you'd reminded me this morning,' I told her. 'Then I'd probably still have my own eyebrows!'

She gave me a very odd look. 'I'm not sure what eyebrows have to do with anything, Lottie, but I remind you ALL the time that it's best to do your homework as soon as you get it – then you wouldn't have to stay up late and rush it.'

'Mum, NO ONE does their homework as soon as they get it. You have to leave it until the last day – it's the law!'

'Fine – just don't expect any sympathy from me when you are up until midnight!'

URGH.

I wish she'd have a glass of wine or something. She's intolerable without Sauvignon Blanc.

9.13 p.m.

I've done my maths and English homework, but I still have geography, French and science to go. I'm feeling so tired and sorry for myself that I could really do with some sympathy right now. I've been huffing and puffing and banging my desk pretty loudly but not a single person has come to check if I am OK – why are my parents so mean?! AND I don't even have any good snacks as they are all in the bin!!

I think homework should be made illegal; I mean, we work hard enough in school, for goodness' sake. Making us work at home too is like child labour. I might start one of those change.org online petitions. Apparently, if you get enough signatures, they have to discuss it in Parliament.

THOUGHT OF THE DAY:
Really glad that eyebrow-manifesting session didn't come good earlier. I was practically imagining a monobrow!!

WEDNESDAY 4 JANUARY

It was after 11 p.m. before I finally got into my bed
last night and getting out of it this morning was
HARD!

Because yoga had made me smash my alarm clock, I
had to rely on Mum waking me up, and she was much
less sympathetic than a snooze button.

The first time she came into my room it felt like it was
the middle of the night. I groaned, rolled over and must
have gone back to sleep, because the next thing I knew
she was shaking me and telling me I only had twenty
minutes to get ready . . . then I must have snoozed off
AGAIN, because all of a sudden she was there bashing
a saucepan against my head and yelling in a not-very-
kind way.

The saucepan thing, as horrible as it was, turned out to be pretty effective at getting me out of bed (don't tell Mum) but the problem is that I only have twelve minutes to get dressed, do my hair and make-up and eat breakfast . . . so I should probably stop writing in my diary and get busy!

7.40 a.m.

OMG, Mum has thrown out ALL the Coco Pops too!!
She tried to give me a bowl of home-made granola
and natural yoghurt that smelt like feet. YUCK. She
also handed me a packed lunch because apparently
eating cheese paninis every single day is not providing
me with the essential vitamins and minerals I need to
grow! I hate this stupid book she's reading!!

We ended up having an argument over how unfair my
life is and now I barely have any time left to draw my
eyebrows on!

7.41 a.m.

Also, I hope this vendetta against Coco the Monkey
ends soon. I'm STARVING.

7.42 a.m.

I think the eyebrows may be a bit too high!! I look a bit
like I've just had a nasty shock, but hopefully no one
will notice.

Just got the hammies out for a quick goodbye. Put Professor Squeakington down on my desk briefly and he weed ALL over my French homework. I tried to mop it off, but there is a rather obvious yellow stain right in the middle of the page. ARGH!! It's too late to redo it, so I hope I don't get into trouble.

7.47 a.m.

Just remembered my earmuffs. My new status as a STYLE ICON starts today!

4.45 p.m.

Got some funny looks and whispers on my way to school, but that's kinda normal for me so I didn't feel that worried. I assumed people were probably just jealous of my earmuffs.

When I walked into our form room though, I realized something was obviously wrong as the whole class burst out laughing. Amber looked up and shrieked,

OMG, Lottie — do you have a death wish or something?!

then she took off her coat, put it over my head and manhandled me straight to the girls' toilets. It was very distressing; I could barely breathe.

'Why are you kidnapping me?' I gasped when I was finally de-coated in cubicle three.

'Lottie, what on earth were you thinking?' she said. 'Didn't you walk to school with Jess, Molly or Poppy?'

'No, I didn't see them.'

'Where are they?!'

'I dunno. Probably running late, I guess.'

She took her phone out and frantically WhatsApped the rest of the gang.

TQOEG WhatsApp group:

> **AMBER:** URGENT RE LOTTIE. MEET IN SCIENCE-BLOCK TOILETS. CUBICLE 3.

> **MOLLY:** OMG! What's happened? Is she OK?

POPPY: Is she hurt? Is she dead??

JESS: I only saw her yesterday . . . She was alive then!!

AMBER: Stop asking pointless questions. Just get here – now!

ME: Hi, it's me. I'm fine BTW.

AMBER: Shut up, Lottie. You are NOT FINE.

The gang arrived in about thirty seconds flat – pretty speedy IMO. They were obviously relived to see that I was still a living being. However, I could tell from the looks on their faces that there was clearly another problem.

'Does someone want to tell me what's wrong?' I asked.

'Umm . . . your –' Molly trailed off and made vague gestures around my face.

'It's just . . . I think –' started Poppy.

Amber sighed and opened the cubicle door. 'Let's just show her,' she said, pushing me forward towards a basin. I reluctantly looked into the mirror, immediately wishing I hadn't . . .

'I'm sorry, Lottie, but you look like a walking advert for McDonald's,' said Jess.

She was right. My eyebrows bore an uncanny resemblance to the iconic Golden Arches, and the earmuffs were the icing on the cake (or the special sauce on the Big Mac, tee hee).

The next thing I knew the tap was running and my head was being pushed into the basin.

'Wash them off,' instructed Amber, who was already getting out make-up from her backpack.

A few minutes later, Amber had worked her magic again and we made our way back to our form room, just in time for the register – phew.

Mr Peters looked up as we came rushing in. 'Glad you could make it, ladies,' he said.

'Sorry, sir,' the five of us muttered.

'It was Lottie's fault,' said Poppy. 'She wanted to grab a McDonald's breakfast.' That made the entire class laugh, and Mr Peters looked very confused.

What do you think my new nickname was for the rest

of the day? Maccy D's. People kept singing '*I'm lovin' it*' every time I walked past, which is particularly annoying when your mother has turned into an anti-UPF warrior and you could murder a burger.

By lunchtime, I was ravenous. I opened my lunchbox, desperate to sink my teeth into my usual cheese-and-ham roll, only to find it had been replaced with a salad complete with an ultra-embarrassing motivational note!

SO EMBARRASSING!!

I tried to scrunch it up and stuff it in my pocket before anyone saw, but Amber grabbed it and read it out to the table. 'How old does she think you are – FIVE?!' she said with a smirk.

I blushed. I'm not sure which was worse: the salad or the note.

'What even is quinoa?!' asked Poppy.

'I don't know, but it looks like something you might find floating on the top of a fish tank,' said Jess.

Molly laughed. 'Mmmmm, fish-tank scum and vegetables – my fave!'

'Thanks, guys,' I said, putting the lid back on my lunchbox. 'Now it's even less appealing.'

Luckily, my friends, who are more concerned with my welfare than my own mother, all pitched in to help me out. Amber bought me a portion of chips, Molly gave me half a Twix, Jess gave me three Monster Munch (v gen!!), and Poppy let me share her satsuma.

After school, I practically jumped out of my skin when Daniel and Theo appeared right in front of my face.

'LOTTIE!' they were shouting.

'What?! What's wrong??' I asked.

'Nothing,' said Daniel. 'But we've been calling your name out for ages.'

'Ahh, I see,' I said, tapping my earmuffs. 'These things make it harder to hear.'

Daniel grinned. 'I like them – they're cute.'

'And now the new nickname makes much more sense,' said Theo, laughing.

Jess appeared at my side, giggling. 'Yeh, it was absolutely nothing to do with the eyebrow malfunction.'

'The eyebrow malfunction?' said Daniel, looking confused.

'It happens to the best of us,' I explained.

'Does it?!'

'No,' I said, laughing. 'I guess it's probably just me.'

PS I tried to apologize to Madame Beaufoy about the yellow stain (I even explained it in French!) but she thought I was being cheeky and made me stay behind and rewrite it during break – BOO.

THURSDAY 5 JANUARY

'I have come up with a resolution!' Toby announced proudly at dinner (tofu and bean casserole – somebody help me, please!!)

'Great,' said Dad. 'What is it?'

'Hopefully, it's to stop farting on me,' I said.

'No, that would be impossible,' said Toby. 'My New Year's resolution is . . .' He paused in anticipation and then proudly announced:

OOOOOOOOH, INTERESTING!

'That's not exactly a resolution,' explained Dad. 'That's just something you want.'

'It doesn't matter what it is, because we are NOT getting a dog,' said Mum.

'Why not?' I asked. 'TBH I think it's one of the best ideas that Toby has ever had.'

Toby grinned. 'Thanks, sis!'

'Erm, well, there are a million and one reasons, but mostly it boils down to the fact that I have enough on my plate to deal with without adding a dog into the mix,' Mum replied with a sigh.

'But you wouldn't have to do anything,' argued Toby. 'I would look after it!'

'And me,' I agreed. 'I'd be the most responsible dog owner ever.'

'I mean, I have to admit, I've always fancied the idea of a four-legged friend . . .' said Dad. 'Let us think about it.'

'We most certainly will not think about it, Bill,' said Mum. 'Sorry, kids – it's not happening.'

'Awwwwwww – I never get anything,' moaned Toby.

'You never get anything?!' spluttered Mum. 'What about that brand-new gaming computer you got for Christmas?'

Toby sighed and stropped off. I excused myself too and followed him.

'Hiiiiiiisssssssss, Toby!'

'What?' he asked, looking miserable.

'It's a great idea, it really is. I think, if we work together, we can convince Mum and Dad that a dog would be amazing! What do you think?'

He looked at me thoughtfully. 'I guess it's worth a shot.'

'Excellent,' I said. 'Now we just need to come up with a clever plan . . .'

'Leave it with me!' said Toby, suddenly much more cheerful. Then he gave me a high-five and ran off to his room.

THOUGHT OF THE DAY:

I couldn't stop thinking about the idea of a pet dog for the rest of the evening. Just imagine all the fun we could have! Frolicking in fields, snuggling in front of the fire, play-ing ball on the beach . . . Ooooh, I could even train it to dance and go on Britain's Got Talent and maybe win a hundred grand!

FRIDAY 6 JANUARY

Fell over on the way to school, probably because I have
no energy now that Coco the Monkey has been banned
from our household so he can't make my milk go all
chocolatey. It was super embarrassing – especially as
I tripped over absolutely nothing and then went flying
across the ground. I tried to style it out and ended up
doing a forward roll down a grassy verge and into the
gutter. It was 8.15 a.m. (peak commuting time) so loads
of people were around.

'OMG, did you see that – it was SO funny!' I heard
someone shriek.

I looked up and saw Candice from Eight Yellow,
standing across the road. She was laughing and
pointing me out to everyone else.

I was in a lot of pain, but I didn't want them to see me
cry, so I pretended that I thought it was funny too. It
would have been OK if I was with someone, but I was
all on my lonesome. I got up and walked away as fast
as I could, even though my ankle was really hurting.

It turned out to be not ALL bad, because Poppy came running up to me and the rest of TQOEG at break. 'Lottie, guess what just happened!'

'What?!'

'I heard something EXCITING in geography!'

'Really? We're learning about irrigation systems and it's not exactly –'

'Obviously not from the teacher – duh. TUMGG were chatting about you!'

'TUMGG?!'

'The Ultimate Mean Girl Gang,' she explained. 'AKA Candice and Izzy G – they're fairly new on the scene.'

'Can you even have a gang if there are only two of you?'

'Well, apparently they are trying to recruit members. They're on a mission to be the meanest girls in the WHOLE school.'

'What?!' said Amber, looking envious. 'Do they seriously think they can out-mean-girl ME?!'

Poppy nodded. 'Well, yesterday, they flushed a Year Seven's pencil case down the loo for being too babyish. It blocked the pipes and Mrs McCluskey had to get a plumber in – she was dead annoyed when the plumber found a pink fluffy axolotl down there. I heard the Year Seven got detention for a whole week!'

Amber raised her eyebrow in appreciation. 'Cool.'

'That's not "cool", Amber – that's mean!' said Jess crossly.

'I think that's the point,' said Amber. 'If they don't do mean stuff, then they may as well call themselves the Ultimate Nice Girl Gang.'

'I think that's actually a great name for a gang,' said Molly.

Amber sighed. 'You would.'

'Anyway,' Poppy went on, 'back to my point – I overheard TUMGG chatting about Lottie! Candice said, "Did you see that girl fall over outside school this morning? It was hilarious." Then Izzy G said, "No, who was it?" and Candice replied, "You know – the one with the childish burger earmuffs," and Izzy G said, "OMG, I think her name is Lottie – that girl is SO cringe."' Poppy grinned at me. 'Isn't that great?'

'Umm . . . not really!'

'Don't you see? Your signature look is actually working! People are starting to recognize you for it!'

'OH, YEH,' I said, grinning.

Amber rolled her eyes. 'Great news,' she said sarcastically. 'Now you just need to work on not being so cringe and childish.'

Way to burst my bubble!

'Thanks,' I said, equally sarcastically.

'Amber – Lottie can't help that. Being cringe and childish is just part of her personality,' said Poppy.

'What is this? Get at Lottie Day?!' I asked.

'But we love you for it,' said Molly, smiling at me.

'And anyway . . . it's not just you,' reassured Jess. 'Our whole gang is pretty cringe and childish – in fact, maybe we should change our name to the Cringe and Childish Gang.'

We all burst out laughing . . . except Amber.

'Speak for yourselves!' she huffed. 'Sometimes I really do think you guys could do with growing up a bit! Then she picked up her bag and walked off.

THOUGHT OF THE DAY:
What's got into Amber lately?! Are we really that cringe and immature?! I mean, I guess she is the most mature of the group, but that doesn't mean that she can boss us about. Sometimes it feels like she thinks she's in charge of us, but I don't remember anyone making her the group leader!

SATURDAY 7 JANUARY

9.22 a.m.

IT HAS NOW BEEN SIX WHOLE DAYS SINCE I HAVE HAD A KITKAT CHUNKY!

Let that sink in.

I honestly don't know if I've ever been this long without a KitKat IN MY LIFE – well, maybe when I was a baby or something?! It's been a VERY long time anyway. I could honestly murder one right now. I mean, not literally – that would be awful and a total waste.

10.11 a.m.

Our entire house smells of farts. OK, that's not entirely unusual – but it's worse than ever now that Mum has us all on a diet largely consisting of beans, lentils and vegetables.

My family members are tooting and parping left, right and centre – me included (shhhh, don't tell anybody).

And the smell is **HIDEOUS**. I don't understand how – if these so-called 'whole foods' are so good for you – they come 'out' (if you get what I mean) smelling so deadly. EWWW.

Anyway, enough of farts, because today is DATE DAY! DATE DAY! DATE DAY!

Not sure why I felt the need to say that three times, but there you go. I mean, it's probably because I've never been to the cinema with a boy before (not counting Toby or my dad, obvs).

One good thing about a cinema date is that it will mostly involve sitting on a seat and listening to other people talk, so there is less opportunity for me to say or do something stupid. If you've been reading about my **EXTREMELY EMBARRASSING** life for the last year and a half, I think you will know why I see this as a MAJOR plus point.

There are a few minor things to worry about though:

1. Snack etiquette – should I bring snacks with me or buy snacks there? Would we share or buy our own? What

type of popcorn does Daniel like – sweet or salty??
Personally, I like a sweet and salty mix and if we
are sharing, and he doesn't like sweet and salty,
what happens then?! If our popcorn preferences
are misaligned, then is there any hope for our
relationship at all???

2. Movie choice – I don't even know what we are
seeing! What if it's too scary and I end up screaming
or hiding under my seat? What if it's super sad and
I end up bawling my eyes out in front of Daniel and
snotting everywhere?

3. Holding hands – are we meant to hold hands during
the movie or not? What if he goes to take my hand
and it's all sweaty and then he immediately regrets
it. What if he has to sit through the WHOLE film
holding my sweaty hand because he is too polite to
let go?

Now I've written them all down, they don't sound that
minor – they sound more major. Especially number three.
Oh god, what if he dumps me because of it and then the
whole school finds out and I get ANOTHER awful nickname!

5.03 p.m.

I'm home!!

Soooooo, I assume you are absolutely desperate to find out how it went, so I'll start from the beginning.

When I arrived, Daniel was already in the foyer and he seemed kinda worried. He doesn't usually look worried, so then I got worried that maybe he wasn't looking forward to our date at all and that maybe he was regretting asking me out, full stop.

I walked up to him nervously. 'Is everything OK,' I asked.

'I've done something stupid, 'he replied. 'I got the film times wrong and, uh, the shark movie isn't on until later. The only thing they have showing now is –' he shifted awkwardly from foot to foot – '*Sing Two.*'

I wanted to jump up and down with joy a bit like I'd drawn in pic 1 . . .

However, I was also trying to be cool, so I responded as per pic 2.

He looked mega relieved. 'Shall we get some popcorn then?'

I smiled. 'Sure – what kind of popcorn do you like?'

'I'm happy to get whatever, but I usually have sweet and salty mix.'

'SAME!'

I think I shrieked a bit too loudly but I was so pleased that our popcorn tastes were in harmony that I couldn't help myself.

We went over to the counter and ordered a large popcorn and two Cokes. Daniel offered to pay, but I insisted, seeing as he'd already bought our tickets, and I wanted to make sure I was being an excellent feminist.

Then we went and found our seats. It was pretty full of kids TBH, but luckily we found a quieter area on the left towards the back, and we sat down and waited for the film to start. I usually try to save the popcorn until after the commercials, but it smelt amazing, so we both agreed to start eating it right away while it was still warm.

I'm not usually a massive fan of sharing food, because I get a bit too stressed about the scenarios:

* Scenario 1: Person you are sharing with eats really quickly and you have to match their pace to make sure you get your fair share and then end up feeling annoyed when there is no popcorn left five minutes later.

* Scenario 2: Person you are with eats really slowly and you are super conscious of looking greedy, so you have to concentrate really hard on not stuffing your face.

* Scenario 3: The person you are sharing with eats at exactly the same pace as you, so the popcorn is shared fifty-fifty and no one ends up feeling stressed or angry.

An example of a Scenario 1 person is Toby: he is the

worst person to share snacks with in the ENTIRE WORLD. This is exacerbated by the fact that I think he doesn't wash his hands after going to the toilet (BLURGH).

An example of a Scenario 2 person is Poppy: she gets too distracted and then forgets about the snacks – I mean, HELLO??? Who forgets about snacks?!

When there are snacks involved, I am LASER-focused on the task of consuming them. It's one of my core life skills, if you can call it a life skill.

An example of a Scenario 3 person is Jess: like Mary Poppins, she is practically perfect in every way, and our greed levels are in complete sync with each other. That's what makes a true BFF.

Anyway, back to the point I was trying to make. I was obviously quite concerned about how Daniel was going to consume the popcorn, so I was hoping he would go first. When he looked at me and said, 'You go first,' I said, 'No, you go first,' and it went on like that for a while, until we finally reached our hands into the box at the exact same time and touched fingers. **EEEEEEE** – the spark!!!

So, now let's get on to the actual watching-of-the-film part . . .

If you haven't already gathered, I LOVE *Sing* – and, even though it's rare for a sequel to be as good, I love *Sing* 2 just as much (possibly more). However, I didn't really want Daniel to know that I was, in fact, a seven-year-old masquerading as a teenager! So I had to be careful about how I reacted to some of my favourite scenes and jokes.

It quickly became clear that I needn't have bothered though, because Daniel let out a big snort when Miss Crawley's eyeball fell out and she replaced it with an apple. I turned to him and burst out laughing. He looked pretty sheepish.

'It's cringey, I know, but some bits are slightly funny.'

I smiled at him. 'Do you want to know a secret? I actually love this movie.'

'Are you serious? I was trying to look like I thought it was super childish.'

'Ha ha, yes – you can drop the act now! Let's just enjoy it, huh?'

'Deal!'

It was much more fun after that, and every time one of my favourite parts came up, I took a sideways glance at Daniel and he was laughing even more than I was.

Towards the end of the film, which I had become totally engrossed in, I felt Daniel's hand reach over into my lap and pick up my hand. I gave his hand a little squeeze to let him know that it was OK with me, and we sat like that, holding hands, until the credits came on. My hands were a bit hot and greasy from the popcorn, but so were his – he didn't seem to mind, so neither did I. It was actually kinda nice. Or maybe REALLY nice.

5.23 p.m.

I wasn't going to tell you this, because I was a little bit embarrassed, and I thought perhaps if I never thought about it again maybe it would be almost like it never happened. But I just have to tell someone, and I think I'd rather write it down here than confide in a real-life person.

OK. Here goes . . .

About ten minutes before the end of the film, I realized I really needed a fart. Like REALLY bad. I tried holding it in, but it was getting uncomfortable. I was noticeably fidgeting in my seat and was worried Daniel would notice. The only thing to do was let it out, so very discreetly I lifted a bum cheek and slowly released the air.

Then, there in the dark, I said a prayer to the God of Farts . . .

Please, please, God of Farts — let it be a quiet odourless one!

Did he answer?

He did not. 🙁

If Tobes had been here, he would have called it a 'real spicy one' and given me a high five, but unfortunately he was not and I had just done one of the **WORST FARTS OF MY LIFE** while sitting next to my boyfriend of a week!!

I could feel my cheeks burning red and I was very glad that it was dark. I started to weigh up my fart-response options:

1. Ignore it.

2. Admit it was me.

3. Blame it on somebody else.

Number 1 wasn't really an option, because it was SOOO
bad and also one of those farts that lingered on FOREVER.

Option 2 – errrrr NO WAY!! It's like our second-ever
date. I don't want him knowing that I fart!

So, we had to roll with Option 3.

Sozzo, Daniel, but you left me with very little choice?!
Ha ha.

6.42 p.m.

Filled in the Fun Police on my date (not the fart bit) and
I told them how fun it had been and how much I liked
Daniel – BIG mistake!!

They said I should invite him round to our house after
school one day this week, as it would be nice to 'meet
him properly'. I reminded them that they'd already met
him multiple times and they said that those were just in
passing and they'd like to be 'formally introduced'.

I said, 'Stop talking in Victorian speak – what do you even
mean?'

'I mean, he could pop over for a cup of tea,' explained Mum.

'Tea?! He doesn't drink tea!'

'He can drink whatever he likes,' said Mum. 'I just think
it would be nice to have a proper chat and get to know
him a bit better.'

'I go to school with him, and he's called Daniel. What else could you possibly need to know?!' I asked.

'Look, Lottie,' said Dad. 'If this lad is your boyfriend and you're going to be going out with him, then your mum and I would like to make sure he's not some sort of . . . serial killer.'

What on earth was he on about?!?!?!

I sighed. I didn't like it, but what choice did I have? 'OK, I'll ask him when he's free.'

'Great!' replied Mum, looking excited, which was worrying for me.

THOUGHT OF THE DAY

I really like hanging out with Daniel, mostly because when I let him see the true me, he doesn't get put off at all – in fact, it seems as if it makes him like me more! What a weirdo!

Now I've just got to hope, hope, hope my family behave when he comes round and meets them all!

SUNDAY 8 JANUARY

Toby knocked on my door early this morning. I
assumed it was to expel some offensive bodily gas,
so I shouted 'GET OUT!' at him.

He said, 'Shhhhh, I have a plan, but I don't want Mum
and Dad to hear.' Then he went on to explain what he'd
come up with. TBH I was pleasantly surprised!

I'll fill you in on the plan later, because right now we
have a lot of work to do.

12.21 p.m.

Me and Toby spent all morning slaving away on our project
and by lunchtime it was ready. I wanted to seem all profesh,
so I suggested we wear our school shirts and smartest
trousers. Toby was quite reluctant but agreed in the end
(although he refused to change out of his rather manky
trackie Bs). Next, I set up my laptop on the kitchen table,
put out glasses and a jug of water, and filled snack bowls
with peanuts and some slightly mouldy-looking olives I
found in the back of the fridge. Then I summoned the rest of

86

the household to join us 'for an important family meeting'.

Mum and Dad seemed very suspicious. 'I'm not sure I like this,' said Mum. 'What's going on?'

I cleared my throat. 'Myself and my esteemed colleague have prepared an insightful, aspiring and illuminating presentation for you, and we are very grateful that you have taken time out of your busy schedules to be here with us today. Please help yourself to refreshments and we will begin in approximately thirty seconds.'

'What's the presentation about?' asked Dad, helping himself to a handful of peanuts.

'It's about something that would enhance all our lives,' I explained.

'It's about getting a dog!' said Toby.

'TOBY!!' I shrieked. 'You've ruined it.'

'We aren't getting a dog, and that is that,' said Mum.

I sighed loudly. This was NOT going to plan. 'Can everybody be quiet? We'd like to begin.'

I clicked to start the slideshow . . .

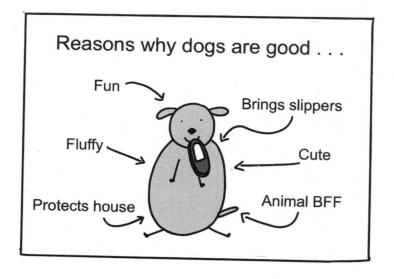

Our final slide was my favourite: we needed to leave them with a strong and emotive message that basically made them feel super guilty.

Then Toby got his harmonica out and started playing a really slow, sad tune, and I tried to look as miserable as possible. I was really pleased because I willed myself to cry so hard that a real tear came out. It was an Oscar-winning performance.

Dad started to clap. 'That was really great, guys – I'm sold!'

Me and Toby jumped for joy.

Mum, however, did not look at all pleased. 'Bill?! What on earth are you saying? I've already made it very clear that we are NOT getting a dog.'

'ORSEY!' shouted Bella, trying to grab my laptop.

It took me a few seconds to work it out, but then it suddenly became clear. 'She thinks the dog is a horse! She wants a dog too, don't you, Bella?'

Bella clapped. 'ORSEY! ORSEY!' she shouted.

'It's four votes to one, Mum,' said Toby. 'Admit defeat!'

Mum stood up and started clearing the table. 'I'm not admitting anything. The fact remains that neither of you are responsible enough to look after a dog.'

'Oh, yes we are!' said me and Toby in unison.

'Oh, NO you're not!' replied Mum.

'Oh, yes we are!'

'Oh, no you're not!'

'OH, YES WE ARE!'

'Is anyone else feeling a bit like they're at a panto?' said Dad.

Everyone ignored him.

'Mum, pleeease,' said Toby. 'We *are* responsible – let us prove it.'

Mum looked thoughtful. 'Hmmm . . . Maybe I have an idea . . .'

I would usually have taken this as a good sign. However, I did not like the way she was smirking and stroking her chin like an evil genius when she said it.

(**1.15 p.m.**)

So it turns out that Mum's idea was messaging the street WhatsApp group that me and Toby were offering a FREE dog-walking service today!

Guess how many people replied – FIVE! It turns out

that on a cold, grey January afternoon, free dog-walking services are pretty popular.

'I wish you'd have said we were charging,' I moaned.

'Yeh, we could have made about fifty quid!' said Toby.

'But it's not about the money, is it?' Mum smiled at us both. 'It's about proving you can be responsible dog owners. Now, make sure you wrap up warm – it's only two degrees out there today.'

There was nothing else we could say to that, so we just smiled sweetly back.

GRRRRRR – not sure I like this evil genius mum.

3.22 p.m.

I'm home. Well, I got home about twenty-five minutes ago, but I had to thaw my fingers by the radiator before I could use them to write.

First things first – **I DO NOT RECOMMEND**

WALKING FIVE DOGS AT ONCE.

This is who we had:

Frank – Labrador

Megazord – Chihuahua

Lulu – White fluffy thing ?!

pedro – Poodle

Sausage – Dachshund

We left Mum at home with her feet up by the fire, and Dad helped me and Toby get them to the park. Then guess what happened . . .

Dad handed his leads to me and Toby, and said ' Right, good luck, guys. I'm not freezing my *rude word* off out here – I'm off to sit in the cafe with a nice cup of coffee.'

So it was just me, Tobes and five dogs.

Then Toby said, 'Oh, cool! Alex is over there on the swings!' With that, he handed me his leads and ran off to join his mate.

So then it was just me and five dogs!! Have you ever tried holding five dogs at once? Because it is NOT easy.

Especially when they are all trying to go in different directions, and one is having a wee (against some poor random person's backpack – eek)!

Next Lulu started doing a poo, and it was like she'd started a trend, as the other four all began doing poos too!

OMG, I had to pick them ALL up, because that is what responsible dog-owner people do.

It was the first time I had ever picked up a dog's poo. GROSS! You can feel it all warm and squishy through the bag – and the SMELL! My eyes were actually watering, and I had to work really hard on not being sick.

But what was I meant to do? I couldn't get Dad to help, as he would tell Mum that I wasn't mature enough to have a dog, and Toby was being about as much use as a chocolate teapot.

There was only one thing for it – I texted my bestie . . .

ME: SOS! In Hove Park with five dogs. Can you help me??

JESS: OOH! Sounds FUN! On my way x

PHEW! While I waited for her, I finished picking up the poops and untangled myself from the leads. By the time she arrived, ten minutes later, I was feeling much more in control.

'Oh, they are sooooo adorable,' she said, running over and patting them all on their heads. 'I thought you said you had five though?'

'Yep, I do.'

'Well . . . I can only see four . . .'

'No, it's definitely five,' I said, counting them out for her. 'One, two, three, four and . . .'

Jess grabbed me by the shoulders. 'Lottie, focus. We'll get to the bottom of this. Now, I'll need you to answer a few questions for me.' She rifled through her bag, took out a notepad and pen, and cleared her throat. 'Where was Megazord when you last saw him?'

'He was right here, next to me!' I said, pointing at the grass.

'And what does he look like?'

'He looks like a dog!'

'Can you be any more specific?'

'Um, um, um . . . a little white dog . . . He was a . . . a Chihuahua!'

'Good. And what was he wearing?'

'Erm . . . oh no, I can't remember! What *was* he wearing?! Oh, oh, oh, I know – fur!'

'Right . . .' She tapped her pen against her lips. 'Did you notice anything peculiar about his behaviour before he went missing?'

'Not really. He did a poo and then just sort of . . . stood there.'

'Hmm, was he having any difficulties at home? Any problems at doggy day care? Friendship issues, that sort of thing?'

'Not that I know of.' I was starting to grow quite impatient. 'Shouldn't we actually start looking for him now?'

'I'm going to have to ask you to calm down, madam. I'm just trying to build an accurate timeline of events. Can you think of any reason why he might run away?'

'Officer – I mean, Jess – I don't mean to be rude, but you've obviously been reading far too many murder mysteries. I think that the best way to look for a lost dog is probably by actually looking for him and calling his name.'

'OK, soz, Lotts! You're right – let's get to work!'

Jess took a couple of the dogs' leads and we ran around the park shouting 'MEGAZORD!' and asking people if they had seen a lost-looking Chihuahua, but nobody had. He seemed to have disappeared into thin air.

After two circuits of the park, I was completely out of breath. 'Jess, what if we never find him?' I puffed.

My mind started to race . . . How was I ever going to convince Mum and Dad that I could be a good dog owner if I had lost a dog within minutes of looking after it?! What was I going to tell poor Megazord's owners?

'We're going to find him, Lottie. I think we've got to be a bit more strategic with our search,' said Jess.

'What do you mean?'

'I mean, what would you do if you were a lost dog?'

'I've no idea!'

'Hmm . . . ' Jess looked thoughtful and then started sniffing. 'Ooh, can you smell that – it's bacon!'

'Yes, but we don't have time to stop for food, Jess.'

'I know that, Lottie – I'm trying to think like a dog. If I was Megazord, I would probably follow that smell to the cafe!'

'Jess, you are SO smart! I bet that's exactly where he is.'

So we ran (with all the other dogs) to the cafe. Even though it was a cold day, it was very busy with lots of people at the outdoor tables, huddled up with hot chocolates, coffees, teas and toasties.

I saw Dad smiling to himself and rubbing his hands as a waitress put what looked like a big bacon and egg bap down in front of him. *I bet he won't tell Mum about that*, I thought to myself!

Jess grabbed my arm excitedly and pointed, 'Lottie, look – there he is!'

I looked over and saw Megazord sitting under a table, eating chips a toddler was dropping off his plate. (He was clearly having a great time.)

'YES!' I jumped up and down. I made a dash to grab him, but he saw me coming and ran off.

He was heading towards Dad, or – more to the point – Dad's sandwich. **EEEEEEK!**

'We've got to stop him! Dad can't see that he got loose,'
I said to Jess as we chased after him – which FYI is
pretty hard to do when you are holding two dogs each
and there is food everywhere.

Unfortunately, we were not quite fast enough and
Megazord leapt up at Dad, just as he was about to take
a bite of his bap, knocking it out of his hand and on to
the floor (he has a surprising amount of power for a
little guy).

'YOU LITTLE –'

I interrupted him before he could finish his sentence.
'Dad, there are children around!'

'RASCAL!'

Dad looked a fifty-fifty mix of sad and angry while we
all watched Megazord, and the rest of the pups tuck
into the – I'll admit – delicious-looking sarnie. It lasted
approximately 0.08 seconds.

Sandwich
Somewhere
inside
here

'Lottie, what on earth is going on? Why weren't you holding his lead?' asked Dad crossly.

'I, err . . . I think I must have dropped it . . . briefly . . .'

He put his hands on his hips. 'Well, that's not exactly showing that you are responsible enough for a dog, is it? I don't think Mum –'

'Please don't tell Mum,' I pleaded.

'Well, I can't exactly lie to her, can I?'

I had no choice but to pull out the big guns. I put my hands on my hips and said, 'If you tell Mum that I lost – I mean, *very briefly* let go of Megazord, then I'll tell her that you left me and Toby on our own so you could eat a bacon and egg bap at the cafe!'

Dad looked crestfallen. 'But I didn't even get to eat it . . .'

'But you wanted to, so it's the same thing. And I think Mum's cooking a delicious bean-and-lentil casserole for tea, so she wouldn't be very happy to hear you'd ruined your appetite on such an unhealthy snack, would she?'

He knew I had him right where I wanted him.

He looked sadly at the dogs, who were all licking the remnants of that lovely-looking bacon sarnie off their lips. 'OK, fine. But can I at least get another bap?'

'Deal,' I said. 'As long as you get one for me too.'

'And me, please!' said Jess.

'And me!!' said Toby, appearing behind me.

'Where have you been?!' I asked him crossly. 'You were meant to be helping me with the dogs!'

'OOPS,' he said as he bent down and started patting Megazord's head. 'Hello, have you been a good boy?'

I glared at him, and Jess burst out laughing.

When we'd finally returned all the dogs to their very grateful owners (several tried to pay us, but Dad wouldn't let them – grrrr!), we got home to find Mum waiting at the window for us.

'So, how was it?' she asked with a knowing smile.

'It was great, actually,' I replied confidently.

'Really?' she said. Clearly she expected it to have gone badly (which it did, but obvs we weren't going to let her know that).

'Yes, we had a REALLY fun time,' I said.

She looked confused. 'Toby? Bill?'

Dad and Toby looked at Mum and repeated: 'We had a REALLY fun time.'

I grinned. 'Looks like we're getting a dog then, aren't we?'

Mum sighed. 'I wouldn't get too excited. It won't be that easy finding a rescue dog that suits a young family, and expensive puppies are out of our budget right now.'

'But if we find one, we can have it?' asked Toby excitedly.

'I suppose so,' she said, looking defeated.

I gave Toby a high-five and picked Bella up and swung her round. 'We're getting an orsey, Bella!' I told her.

'ORSEY! ORSEY!' she shouted out with glee.

THOUGHT OF THE DAY:
Just in case you are worried, let me tell you that I have NOT forgotten about Toby's abandonment in the park earlier. Mark my word, I WILL get him back for that . . . Revenge is a dish best served cold!

MONDAY 9 JANUARY

Today was a good day. I hung out with Daniel at break time. I shared my tray bake with him, and we held hands in public and everyone kept looking over at us and whispering, but in a nice way, so I kinda enjoyed it! I didn't ask him about meeting my parents yet though – I'm hoping Mum will forget.

At lunchtime I told TQOEG all about our date, and Molly goes, 'You and Daniel are, like, the cutest couple in school at the moment.'

That made me feel V V V happy!

Everyone agreed – except Amber, who rolled her eyes and looked dead bored. I'm getting quite fed up with her rudeness TBH. Poppy still thinks that she doesn't seem her normal self and perhaps there is something wrong that she's not telling us about, but I'm not convinced. I personally think she's just jealous. That's the annoying thing about Amber: she can be a great friend when it suits her, but she can't cope with anyone else getting attention.

In other news, Bella is turning one soon – I can't believe it's been a whole year since I delivered her. I still haven't got my Pride of Britain award or been knighted for it. I mean, the things I had to see, the things I had to do, the bodily fluids . . .

SHUDDER!!

Actually, let's not think about that – I'm trying to block it out. Perhaps I should ask the Fun Police to pay for some therapy?!

Anyway, to celebrate the momentous occasion, Mum is throwing what sounds to be quite an extravagant birthday party for her. Not sure why she's stressing herself out though. I mean, Bella's only going to ONE year old – she won't remember a single thing about it.

Mum's ordered a cake and fancy balloons, planned games AND bought Bella a new party dress. I think it's all very OTT, but who am I to criticize?

None of the family are coming, as we only saw them at Christmas and it's a long way to come from Leeds. Instead, Mum has invited Bella's friends from her playgroup – but I'm not sure if you can really call them friends, seeing as they can't even really speak yet, but whatever. Mum said the other mums in the group are quite 'well to do', so she wants to make a good impression. But if she wants to make a good impression, I've no idea why she has invited them over to the madhouse!

And finally my big news: it has been EIGHT WHOLE DAYS since I have consumed a KitKat Chunky and I am feeling quite proud of myself. Normally when I'm feeling proud, I'd reward myself with a KitKat Chunky, but, er yeh, there are none in the house and I guess that would defeat the point.

TUESDAY 10 JANUARY

What do you want first? The good news or the bad news?

Sorry, I couldn't quite hear that – **DO YOU WANT THE GOOD NEWS OR THE BAD NEWS?**

It's no use. I can't hear you (maybe you should get those ears checked?) so I'll have to flip a coin: heads for good; tails for bad.

Here we go . . .

It's tails!

Pfffffft – OK, it wasn't, and I feel bad for lying to you. It was heads, but I always like the bad news upfront, so that's what I'm gonna do. Sorry for wasting your time.

Bad News 1: For our English homework, we have to research a cause, topic, person or book that interests us and then report back on it with a presentation to the class. Maybe you don't think that sounds particularly bad but, take it from me, it is if you HATE public speaking.

I mean, who enjoys public speaking?!?!

You basically have to stand there while everyone stares at you and wills you to fail, because that's what it's like at secondary school. Your classmates want you to mess up so that they can all laugh at you. I mean, we all remember this classic moment from Year 7, don't we? Urgh – it still makes me want to die of shame.

The only good thing is that we get to do it in pairs, and luckily Miss Dodson said that me and Jess could work together. Everything is always so much better when I have Jess by my side.

Bad News 2: Mum asked me about Daniel coming round for tea – groan. I said I hadn't asked him yet and she gave me a look. I thought she was about to let the subject drop, but then she got all overexcited, like she'd had the best idea ever, and said, 'I know! Why doesn't he come to Bella's birthday?'

I wanted to say, *Erm because it will be total mayhem and it's probably the worst idea you've ever had.*

But then I started to think, *Well, at least the Fun Police will be massively distracted, so hopefully that will mean they don't get a chance to grill Daniel all that much* – so it may actually be an ideal time for them to meet? When I say 'ideal', I mean 'better than average' or 'kind of OK' or 'not totally disastrous' (although TBH it still has a very real chance of being totally disastrous).

Good News 1: There has been a MAJOR new development on the dog front.

Dad told us that at work today he was talking about possibly getting a dog while trying to fix Rodge's computer, and Rodge said that his neighbour Don had got a puppy but unfortunately it turned out that his wife, Karen, was allergic to dog hair and so they were trying to rehome it with another family. Well, Rodge asked Dad if he wanted him to call Don and ask if it was still available, and Dad said yes!! Sooooooo Rodge called Don and they said that if we were interested, we could go and visit the puppy tomorrow!!!!!!!!!!

I LOVE RODGE AND DON AND KAREN!

Although Karen is apparently quite upset about the whole thing as she really liked the puppy. Soz, Karen. #SadTimes

Me and Toby were obvs absolutely delighted by this development, but Mum was . . . not delighted . . . Maybe that's putting it a bit mildly. I think when she agreed that we could get a dog she imagined it would take a bit longer to find one than two days.

She got a bit shouty with Dad in the kitchen, saying stuff like:

'Bill, what on earth were you thinking?!'

'It's Bella's birthday tomorrow! Why would we want to go

and look at a dog?!'

'You should have asked me first!'

'You are totally irresponsible!'

'If I say no, it makes me look like the evil parent, doesn't it?'

'I'm going back to work in a couple of months. Have you even considered that?!'

'What kind of dog even is it?'

After a while she started to get pretty cross . . .

I mean, I'm not even on her side, but I had to agree she made some pretty good points. Dad really should have asked a few more questions about the dog when he spoke to Don. We don't know how old it is, if it's a boy of girl, or even what size it is – it could be a Toy Poodle or a German shepherd!

Not that I care though – any dog would be BRILLIANT!!

Good news 2: My eyebrows are starting to grow back. I mean, they're quite stubbly at the moment, so I don't think I'll be able to ditch the eyebrow pencil for a while yet, but it's progress!

WEDNESDAY 11 JANUARY

Today is Bella's actual birthday, but as we are having a proper party at the weekend, I think it's perfectly reasonable that we push her aside for the moment and focus on what's most important – GETTING A DOG!

We're all super excited about visiting him/her later. Except Mum, obvs. She said, 'We are just going to look at the dog. It is *highly unlikely* we will actually get it.'

LOL.

I don't know what planet she's on, because everybody knows that you don't just go and look at a dog and not get it! I guess maybe if it was a mean, bitey dog, then that might happen, or if it wasn't really a dog at all but a pig. Not sure how you'd think a dog was a pig though. Also, I would actually quite like a baby piglet, so I'd be happy anyway.

Home now. School was dull as usual – I spent all day just waiting to get home because I've been SO excited. Now we're waiting for Dad to get in from work and then we'll be driving over to Don and Karen's house.

OOOOOH, I really hope it's a good dog and that the Fun Police agree that we can have it.

I made a pact with Toby and Bella that if Mum expressed any opposition we should all immediately burst into tears.

6.22 p.m.

We are officially getting the dog!!!!!!!!!

I'll draw you a quick picture – LOOK AT HIS FACE!!

MY NEW DOG*!

*I realize he looks a bit more like a sheep here but he is almost definitely a dog.

Is he (A) cute, (B) uber cute or (C) ridiculously, fantabulously cute?

I'll help you out here – the answer is most definitely C.

So I guess you want to know all the deets, right?

Well, he's a golden cockapoo and he's five months old and he's called Snookums (we are going to change that, but we didn't tell Karen and Don).

I just wanted to die every time I looked at him and I felt like my heart might explode into a million pieces!

Mum did, as expected, try to suggest that we should take more time to think about it, but me, Toby and Bella all immediately burst into tears as planned and she eventually caved – ha ha! I mean, she could hardly disappoint Bella on her birthday, could she?! Although TBH I think Bella was crying because she wanted to attack Don and Karen's TV with a remote control (which is one of her favourite hobbies), but it didn't seem to matter much. We had guilt-tripped/embarrassed Mum into saying yes and that's the main thing. I think the fact that Rodge said he was fully toilet-trained helped to swing it. Dad agreed to work from home more often and we all promised that we'd be really good with picking up poos and taking him out on walks.

The only bad news was that we couldn't actually take the dog home yet, because we need to buy a bunch of stuff like food, a bed, toys and a collar and lead.

We are all excited (expect for Mum, who looks a bit shell-shocked about the whole thing, but it's fine – she'll get used to it). She'll have to – ha ha.

8.35 p.m.

We have all agreed that we need to rename our dog, so after dinner me and Toby had a heated two-hour debate over it. Largely because all he could come up with were names of footballers, F1 drivers or YouTubers.

'How about Harry Kane?' he asked.

'Veto,' I said.

'Lando Norris?'

'Veto.'

'Mr Beast?'

'Veto.'

'You can't just veto EVERYTHING I say!'

'I can if the suggestions are ridiculous!'

'I bet you don't have any better ideas.'

'I do! How about . . . Justin Bieber?'

'Ewwww, veto.'

'How about Tom Holland . . . or Harry Styles?'

'VETO! You can't just name the dog after some celebrity you have a crush on.'

I huffed. 'OK what about Cutesy-Wootsy McPoochy?'

'NO WAY!' shouted Toby.

Dad came into the kitchen and said, 'I really don't mind what you call the hound, but even I draw the line at that one – I mean, can you imagine me walking him in the park and practising recall with that name?'

TBH I really liked that idea, but I guess Dad did have a point.

'Why don't we ask Bella?' said Mum.

We all looked at Bella.

'POO BUM!' she screamed while trying to feed her toast into the DVD player.

Dad laughed. 'Or maybe not!'

'This is hopeless – we're never going to agree,' I said with a sigh.

'LOTTIE BROOKS!' said Mum crossly as she was emptying the kitchen bin. 'Why is there a Pot Noodle in here? I thought I had thrown them all away.'

I had to think quickly on the spot, as I was absolutely not going to tell her about the secret UPF stash under my bed.

'I found it right at the back of the cupboard, and it felt wrong to let it go to waste,' I argued.

Mum sighed. 'And you haven't even emptied the pot out before putting it in the bin!'

'Sorry, Mum,' I said as a trail of chicken-and-mushroom broth dribbled on to the floor and filled the house with a (in my opinion) lovely aroma . . .

Mum dragged the bin bag to the front door, and I was contemplating whether I should get up and help or not, when an idea came to me like a bolt of lightning.

'Mum, you are a genius! I've got it!'

'What?!'

'I know what we should name our dog . . .'

Everyone stopped still. The silence was palpable.

Toby finally spoke: 'Actually, I quite like that.'

'It would suit him,' said Dad, nodding. 'His fur does look quite like noodles.'

'Well, I'd personally rather not name him after a processed food,' Mum huffed. 'What about something a little healthier, like, um . . . aubergine?'

We all stared at her.

'I think I like that even less than Cutesy-Wootsy McPoochy,' said Dad finally.

'Well, that's settled then,' I said, jumping up and clapping. 'Pot Noodle, it is!'

8.51 p.m.

TQOEG WhatsApp group:

ME: I've got the best news ever!

AMBER: You won a million pounds on the lottery?

ME: No.

POPPY: KitKat Chunkys are BOGOF in Sainos?

ME: No. And that would actually make me sad, because I'm not allowed them any more 🙁

JESS: When you sneeze, a tiny bunny comes out of your nose!

AMBER: Jess, that just sounds insane!

ME: I mean, I'd quite like it . . . but it's not correct.

MOLLY: OOH! I know – your eyebrows are growing back!!

ME: No. Well, they are, but that's not THE good news. THE good news is . . .

ME: . . .

ME: . . .

AMBER: You are getting on my nerves now, Lottie.

ME: OK, soz – I'M GETTING A DOG!!!!! 🐕 🐕 🐕

POPPY: ARRRRRRRRRRRGHHHHHHH!

JESS: NO WAY!!!!!

MOLLY: EEEEEEEK!

AMBER: Am I the only one feeling slightly underwhelmed?!

MOLLY: We need details now!

ME: He's a five-month-old cockapoo and he is the cutest dog EVER! I ♥ him.

MOLLY: Does he have a name?

ME: Yep, it's Pot Noodle.

JESS: LOL – love it! 😂

POPPY: BEST NAME EVER!!!

JESS: OMG, I'm so excited for you – and me! Promise we'll get to meet him first!!

ME: I promise! xx

THOUGHT OF THE DAY:

Crikey, imagine being able to sneeze tiny bunnies!

I guess it might seem amazing at first – but it would quickly become quite annoying, wouldn't it? You'd have people following you around with a feather trying to get you to sneeze, just so they could see it happen.

And then . . . what are you meant to do with all those tiny bunnies? I mean, a couple would be fine, maybe three or four, but after that it would become a bit ridiculous, wouldn't it?!

AND you'd have to name them all. Although TBH I'd probably quite like that bit . . .

THURSDAY 12 JANUARY

Told everyone at school about MY new dog. MINE!
Wow, how lovely it is to say that.

I think the girls are almost as excited as me. None of
them have a dog, so I think they're also a bit envious.
Apart from Amber, who said dogs are gross because
they poo everywhere and then they lick their own
bum holes. I guess that is a bit gross, but so are a lot of
things in life, so who cares?

Daniel is really excited as well – he used to have a dog,
but it died. He looked really sad when he told me, and
I thought I might cry, but then he said it lived until it
was thirteen and had a really nice life, so I guess that
it's a kind of happy/sad thing.

After school today, we went to Pets Palace to buy
supplies. Me and Toby argued loads – sometimes I
think he disagrees with everything I suggest just to
wind me up. If I say red, he says blue, and if I change
my mind to blue, he says red. It's **SOOOOOOO**
annoying!

Then the Fun Police started getting really cross and saying stuff like, 'If you're going to keep this up, we'll go home right now and cancel getting Pot Noodle.' That right there was a prime example of an empty threat! In the end, this is what we got:

- ★ Turquoise lead
- ★ Purple harness
- ★ Dog pen
- ★ Red fleece-lined bed
- ★ Water and food bowls
- ★ Puppy pads (for any accidents)
- ★ Raincoat
- ★ Shampoo
- ★ Toothbrush and meaty toothpaste (eww!)
- ★ Lots of cartons of food
- ★ Meaty treats and gravy bones
- ★ Poo bags
- ★ Ball and thrower
- ★ Squeaky burger toy
- ★ Cuddly carrot toy

Dad almost fainted at the till when he saw the total cost. He quickly pulled himself together when Mum raised her eyebrows in an 'I told you so' way.

When we got home, we set up Pot Noodle's pen and bed, and laid out his toys. He's going to be the most-loved and best-looking dog in Brighton. In fact, I might start entering him into dog shows. OMG, what if he won Crufts?! That would be **SO** cool!

PS Mum asked me again whether Daniel was coming to Bella's b-day party. I'd been so caught up with dog excitement that I'd not asked him yet, and TBH maybe I'd been putting it off because it feels a bit grown-up and nerve-racking. What if he doesn't want to? What if he says no? What if he makes up some terrible excuse? What if he says yes and I have to introduce him to my extremely embarrassing family??? ARGH!!!!

PPS Slightly worried that Bella thinks everything we bought from the pet shop today is for her!

FRIDAY 13 JANUARY

I was VERY distracted in school today, which is not at all like me (ahem).

In art, I drew a picture of a poodle. In English, I wrote a poem about a pug who likes giving hugs and sitting on rugs. In history, we had a pop quiz on the French Revolution and I just listed my favourite breeds of dog (not sure I'll do very well). In maths, Mrs Vincent asked me what the square root of 169 was and I barked at her.

I ended up in the medical room after that, and the school nurse asked me if I was feeling OK. I said I thought maybe I was a bit dehydrated, and she gave me a glass of water.

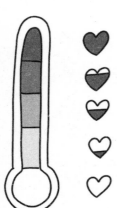

After school, me and Daniel went to Frydays together and shared some cheesy chips – I know what you are thinking . . . *Ding, ding, ding! Lottie's nearly reached the top of the Chipometer of Love and they are practically in lurve!* The girls were all there too, and they giggled when they saw what we had ordered, except for Amber, who looked bored and rolled her eyes, but whatevs – she can be jealous all she likes. I'm not going to let her get to me.

We sat on the bench outside to eat them, huddled up close as it was freezing, and I knew I had to finally ask Daniel if he could come to the party.

'So, I was just wondering . . .' I began. 'I mean, you might be busy anyway, which is fine – it's late notice, so you probably are . . . Or, you know, you might not want to come . . . No pressure or anything – it's cool if you don't . . . If I was you, I probably wouldn't. I would probably rather stick pins into my eyes, or set fire to my toenails, or put a siren on my head and run up and down the road in my underwear shouting "Nee-naw" or –'

'Um, Lottie, not that I'm not enjoying this monologue, but did you want to ask me a question?'

'Oh, errr, yes, I did . . .' I looked at the ground and blurted it out, 'It's Bella's birthday party on Sunday and my mum wants me to ask you if you could come . . . I mean, you're probably busy and –'

'Enough with the monologues! I'd love to come.'

'That's fine – don't apologize. It's late notice and –'

'Lottie, I said I'd love to come!'

'Oh, really? That's great,' I said, smiling.

Even though it was going to create a whole new list of worries in my brain, I was glad that he *wanted* to be there.

'I have one question though,' he said.

'Yeh?'

'If you were me, would you seriously rather run up and down the street in your underwear pretending to be a police car?'

I laughed. 'Maybe . . . You haven't met my family properly yet, remember?'

THOUGHT OF THE DAY 1:
OMG!!!!!!!!!!!!! I cannot believe we are getting a dog tomorrow! I am so happy I wanna die*!!!!!

* Not literally, obvs.

THOUGHT OF THE DAY 2:
I wonder if toenails are flammable . . .

SATURDAY 14 JANUARY

DOG DAY! DOG DAY! DOG DAAAAAAAAAAAAAAAAAAAAAAAAY!

WHEEEEEEEEEEEEEEEEEEEEEEEE!

I don't think I have ever been so excited IN MY LIFE . . . unless you count the time I bit into a KitKat and found out it was solid chocolate all the way through!

That was *very* exciting, but also over in about three minutes because I gobbled it up so quickly.

What won't be over in about three minutes, or gobbled up, is a dog!! Woohoo, soon we are going to collect Pot Noodle and bring him back to his forever home and forever family!

Pot Noodle is here! I think he likes me the best in the family. He sat on my knee on the way home in the car. Toby was not impressed, but he could not be trusted to be sensible with him.

When I put Pot Noodle down on the floor, the first thing he did was run into the living room and do a massive wee on the rug. Mum looked horrified and Dad said, 'Don't worry – it's normal to have a few accidents while we're toilet-training him.'

'I thought he was already house-trained!' said Mum. 'Rodge did say he was fully toilet-trained, didn't he?'

'Yes, of course he did. It's just a new environment, so it may take a day or two to get used to it.'

Introduced PN to the hammies – I'm not sure they
were super keen on him . . .

11.55 a.m.

I tried to play catch with Pot Noodle in the garden,
but he wasn't very good at bringing the ball back.
He seemed to prefer digging holes in the grass. Mum

wasn't very happy when we came back inside because he jumped on the sofa with muddy paws and rolled around, wanting to have tummy tickles. Then he did two more indoor wees: one on the carpet in the hallway and one right next to a puppy pad that Mum had set up by his crate.

I think Mum is already starting to regret agreeing to have Pot Noodle.

12.15 p.m.

Dad keeps taking Pot Noodle outside to do his wees, but Pot Noodle spends the time in the garden barking at everything and digging instead of doing any wees. He seems to get cross about a lot of things, including:

* People talking in other gardens
* Car doors opening and closing
* Other dogs barking
* Cats sitting on walls
* Squirrels in general
* Insects
* Birds flying over our garden
* Our gnomes

I mean, the gnomes aren't even doing anything.
They're just sitting there, minding their own immobile
stone business.

(1.35 p.m.)

OMG, I'm absolutely traumatized by what I've just
seen, and I have seen some terrible things in my short
life, let me tell you that.

Pot Noodle was just . . .

OMG, I'm not sure I want to tell you!

OK, OK, I will. I need to blurt it out.

I FOUND POT NOODLE HUMPING TEDDY ONE-EYE!!

Poor Teddy One-Eye was obviously VERY distressed. Worse still, the hammies saw everything – now they are even less keen on Pot Noodle, and I can't say that I blame them.

BRB – off to wash my eyes out with soap.

(2.57 p.m.)

Oh dear. Mum is cross because Pot Noodle decided to try to eat the sofa. I mean, it's pretty big, so he didn't manage to eat *that* much of it. Just one *smallish* corner. Mum seems to think it's quite a huge problem though. Not sure why – she could just put a throw over it!

(3.22 p.m.)

Posted a pic of me and my pooch on Insta and it got LOADS of comments and likes.

I asked Mum if the girls could come round and meet him, but she seemed

pot Noodle has arrived!
#NEW BFF #pAWSomE
#pAWTYTIME #BESTWOOF
♥ 47 likes
◉ OMG – he's totes adorbs!
◉ I need to meet him NOW!!

a bit stressed out (not sure why) so she said no. They were very disappointed – so was I, as I can't wait to show him off.

5.45 p.m.

EWWWW! I just had to feed Pot Noodle and it was SO disgusting I nearly vommed. Apparently the flavour was 'tripe loaf', which is a lot of horrible dead body parts moulded into a can shape. Mum said I had better not complain about doing it, seeing I was the one who was meant to be the best dog owner in the ENTIRE world.

I didn't know that I'd have to feed him tripe loaf though, did I?!

6.59 p.m.

Mum caught Toby dissecting one of Pot Noodle's poos with a stick. He said it was a scientific experiment and now Mum says that poo duty is one hundred per cent my responsibility because Toby can't be trusted – how is that fair??

7.13 p.m.

Bella keeps chasing Pot Noodle around the house, grabbing his fur and shrieking, 'ORSEY!'

I think Bella and Pot Noodle actually have quite a lot in common: they like to poo and wee everywhere, shout at random things and chew stuff they shouldn't.

OMG, maybe Bella is a dog trapped in a human body?! That would actually make quite a lot of sense.

7.32 p.m.

Just saw Pot Noodle cock his leg and do a wee against Toby's school bag. I'm just going to keep quiet about that one, tee hee.

8.03 p.m.

Catching up on YouTube, and Pot Noodle is all snuggled up in my lap, fast asleep. He deffo likes me best, which I'm thrilled about.

It's been an interesting first day of being a dog owner: there've been some highs and lows, but generally I LOVE it. Not sure the Fun Police are quite so keen though.

Oh, well – hopefully Pot Noodle will sleep very well tonight after his crazy antics today.

(9.15 p.m.)

Bella is having a protest in her cot. She won't go to sleep without Pot Noodle! She's been screaming 'ORSEY!' and banging the bars of her cot for the last hour. I personally think the only solution is to let her sleep with him in the puppy pen. Mum completely disagrees, as she thinks that would be irresponsible and not a habit she wants to get into.

(10.37 p.m.)

After another solid hour of 'ORSEY!' howls, Mum has cracked. She made a bed for Bella in Pot Noodle's puppy pen and is now sitting with them in the kitchen, willing them both to go to sleep. Apparently when Bella goes to sleep, Mum will carry her upstairs to her cot.

11.02 p.m.

Mum is the only one in the puppy pen who has actually fallen asleep.

SUNDAY 15 JANUARY

(8.35 a.m.)

Woke up and remembered we had a dog – YAY. Ran downstairs and gave him some morning tummy tickles.

Apparently Mum hadn't forgotten, as she'd been up half the night with either Bella or Pot Noodle – neither of whom seemed that interested in sleeping. She is very tired, and feeling unenthusiastic about today's party.

I also remembered that Daniel is coming round to meet the fam – **ARGHHH!!!!!!!!**

(9.55 a.m.)

The house is all abuzz. Mum is running around like a headless hoovering chicken, and Dad is putting up decorations and then taking them down again when Mum yells, **'NOT LIKE THAT! IT LOOKS STUPID THERE!'**

IMO she is going way OTT – I mean, who are these other babies? Royalty?! She's made loads of fingers sandwiches, sausage rolls, crudités and various homemade dips (that look like vomit). She's even done party bags. There are pink and gold shiny balloons hanging from the ceiling, as well as bunting and a huge helium number '1' that Bella is trying to fight.

Toby is meant to be looking after the dog, but he is on his iPad, picking his nose, and Pot Noodle just did a massive wee on Mum's party shoes. I'm not sure if I should tell anybody (I probably won't as it's not my fault anyway).

I would love to help, but I'm also super busy thinking about all the stuff I need to do before Daniel arrives. On my to-do list, I currently have:

1. Tidy my room and remove any dirty plates/cups and chocolate/crisp wrappers.

2. Hide any embarrassing paraphernalia (I hope you are impressed by my use of that word) such as Justin Bieber merch, Teddy One-Eye and any stray Sylvanian Families. (I really should get rid of them now I'm a teenager!)

3. Have a shower – my hair is an absolute greaseball and my armpits are slightly whiffy to say the least.

4. Elect a cute (not too 'try hard') outfit to wear.

5. Have a ten-minute meditation session to chill out and reassure myself that the fam meeting my boyfriend for the first time will go super well.

I have three hours to complete all the above so I

should be clean and serene by the time Daniel arrives
– wooooohooooooo!

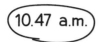

10.47 a.m.

Now Mum is EVEN more stressed out because the cake hasn't arrived yet and she keeps saying, 'You can't have a party without a cake – you just can't!'

Dad offered to go to Tesco and buy one, and she looked at him like he'd grown another head. I'm pretty sure that I got a Colin the Caterpillar for most of my birthday parties, and if it was good enough for me, I'm not sure why it's not good enough for Bella!

Mum says the other mums are quite posh, and they would look down on a Colin the Caterpillar cake. Poor Colin!!

11.09 a.m.

Mum's all dressed and ready – told her she looked lovely. Played dumb about the wee-soaked shoes.

FYI she was wearing clothes here – I just don't have time to draw them. Just telling you that in case you thought she was naked (apart from the wee shoes).

11.22 a.m.

OMG OMG OMGGGGGGGGGGGGGGGGGGGGGGGGGGG!

The hamsters have gone missing!!!!!!!

Bella must have crawled into my room and opened their cage door. Either that or they've run away from home because they're upset about me getting a new pet!

I screamed the entire house down and now everyone is hunting everywhere for them, but so far . . . nothing. Apparently the first twenty-four hours a person goes missing are crucial so please cross your fingers that they are OK!!

Still no sign. I am out of my mind with worry. We have looked everywhere – under all the beds and furniture, in the kitchen cupboards, behind the bookcases. I even made Dad unscrew the panel on the bath in case they'd somehow got into there – but **NOTHING**.

What if I never find them again? What if something has happened to them? OMG, what if Pot Noodle has eaten them?!

12.15 p.m.

'Lottie! Lottie! Daniel's here!' called Mum. It was clearly not the first time she'd shouted that, but I had my head under the bed, so I didn't hear her. I'd also clearly lost track of time because, errrr, I wasn't dressed and I also realized, as I tried to back myself out, that I was totally stuck.

'Hi, Lottie,' Daniel said to my exposed pyjama bottoms.

'Oh, ummm . . . Hi, Daniel. I would get out and say hi to your face, but think I might be . . . kind of trapped.'

I tried shuffling out backwards again, but there was so much stuff under there that I was totally jammed in.

'Right, there's only one thing for it,' said Mum, 'You take one leg, Daniel, and I'll take the other.'

OH, GAWD.

I heard Daniel shuffle from one foot to the other and say shyly, 'Umm, sure, Mrs Brooks.'

'Call me Laura, please.'

'OK, Laura.'

Then I felt two pairs of hands grab me round the ankles – which is when I realized I was wearing my unicorn slippers. I cringed . . . deeply.

'One, two, three – PULL!' instructed Mum.

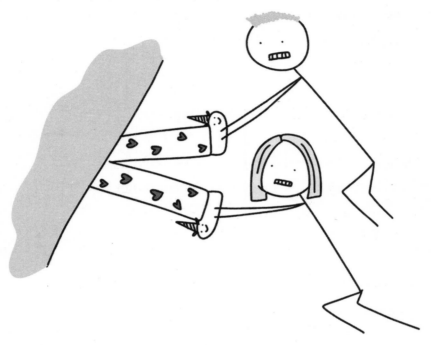

And then I was out, alongside a shoebox of old
Sylvanian Families, which turned over and spilled on
to the floor. I looked fondly at the Bramble Hedgehog
family, who I'd not seen since circa 2017, before I
kicked them back under the bed (I'd apologize later).

'Hi, Daniel,' I said rather awkwardly, because I'd not
had time to do ANY of my prep. My room was a tip, my
hair was greasy (and now covered in dust bunnies),
and I was wearing VERY old and VERY holey PJs.

'Sorry about the mess,' I said, gesturing at my room. 'And sorry I'm not dressed, but there's been an emergency – Professor Squeakington and Fuzzball the Third are missing.'

Luckily, Daniel was almost as alarmed as I was (he was really looking forward to meeting those guys), so while I sprayed myself with dry shampoo/deodorant and got dressed, he helped the rest of the family hunt those naughty hammies down – which I guess was a bonding experience?!

By the time I'd got downstairs, it seemed like Daniel was fully integrated into family life.

'I see you've met Pot Noodle,' I said, looking at my naughty puppy, who was currently humping Daniel's right leg.

'Um, yes . . . He's very –'

'Stop that, Pot Noodle!' I shouted, as I tried to pull him away.

But, dear reader, it did not work. Every time me, Mum or Dad tried to remove Pot Noodle, he ran right back to Daniel.

'He clearly likes you!' joked Dad.

Toby thought the whole thing was hilarious, especially when Bella crawled over and started imitating Pot Noodle's actions on Daniel's left leg.

Poor, poor Daniel.

He was now very red-faced. I did feel sorry for him, but I also kind of enjoyed being the one who was not a deep shade of pink for a change.

Anyway, what with all the commotion, luckily the Fun Police didn't get the chance to grill Daniel too much, so that is one positive. And, um, I think it was definitely an ice-breaker!

Right, I've got to dash. It's only half an hour to go until the party and we **STILL** haven't found the hammies. Everyone kept reassuring me that they'll get hungry and come out of their hiding place eventually, so I'm trying to keep calm and TBF they *are* the greediest hamsters you'll ever meet.

Mum still seems more worried about the lack of cake and the fact that Bella is going ballistic because she hates the ridiculous party dress Mum has forced her to wear. Mum keeps saying stuff like, 'She'll calm down eventually.' and 'She'll get used to it.'

Does she not know that baby at all?!

12.45 p.m.

Bella is not calming down and she is not getting used to it. Bella is practically purple and she is screaming the house down.

I can see Mum debating whether it's better to have her in the dress and screaming or in another outfit and happy.

They're playing a game of chicken with each other, and
me and Toby have made a 50p bet on who wins. I'm on
Team Bella; he's on Team Mum.

(12.55 p.m.)

With minutes to go, Team Bella takes the trophy. She
did a large runny poo that escaped her nappy and now
the dress is ruined and unreturnable. Some might say
it was on purpose and I would have to agree.

Anyway, she is back in her fave Babygro . . .

I can't say I blame her, because her dress looked mega uncomfortable. No one in their right mind would want to wear a dress like that – I don't know what Mum was thinking.

Well, I don't think I'm very keen on Bella's friends! I say 'friends' pretty loosely as none of the babies seemed to like each other very much. There's Harriet, Tamara, Oscar, Matilda and Clive. Yep, you read that right – Clive. Who on earth calls a baby Clive?!

Ahh, isn't he perfect – I think I'll call him Clive!

First, they all gave their presents to Bella, who was not at all grateful. Harriet and Oscar got her books (which she hated), Tamara got her a set of stacking cups (boring), Matilda got her a cuddly giraffe, which Bella threw across the living room and shouted 'NOT!' – she obviously has some sort of issue with giraffes, but your guess is as good as mine. The only successful present was Clive's xylophone, but it was almost too successful as the babies all started a mass fight over who got to play with it first. Even though it was technically Bella's toy, Clive demanded it back and then kept hitting the others on the head with the mallets. He seems incredibly angry for an eighteen-month-old – maybe he doesn't like his name very much either.

The mums were not much better. They spent the whole time boasting about their babies even when (IMO) there was not much to boast about.

They were all like . . .

'Harriet started walking at eight weeks old.'

'Oscar can already count to ten in three different languages.'

'Matilda has the reading age of a seven-year-old.'

Toby said, 'Well, Bella can say "poo" and "bum", can't you, Bella?'

Everybody looked horrified. Mum looked especially mortified and manoeuvred Toby out of the room and said, 'Right, who wants a game of Pass the Parcel!'

Phew – the cakey-bakey lady has delivered the cake! Mum was dead relieved to see her standing on the doorstep holding a big white box. I must admit I was relieved too – hopefully Mum will chill out a bit now.

As Mum was in the middle of trying to make violent babies sit in a circle, I took the cake box from the cakey-bakey lady and brought it through to the kitchen, where I put it on the table.

'Cake's finally arrived!' I said to Dad, who was making cups of tea for the guests.

I lifted off the lid to take a peek and immediately put it back on again.

'Oh God,' I said, letting out a sort of half-laugh, half-gasping sound.

'What's wrong?' asked Dad. 'Is the cake not very good?'

'It's good. It's just a bit, er . . . surprising.'

Dad lifted up the lid and took a look. His eyebrows moved halfway up his forehead – clearly he wasn't expecting this either . . .

'Should we check with Mum?' I asked, suddenly feeling a bit panicky.

'It's probably best not to. She's got enough going on,' Dad advised. 'And I'm sure it's meant as a joke.'

(3.04 p.m.)

The party is over – everyone has gone.

Why is it over so soon? I hear you ask. Weeeeeelllllllllll . . . where to begin? There were a few minor mishaps, I guess.

It all started to go wrong during Pass the Parcel. You see, if you give a bunch of already angry babies a big shiny parcel, they might not be keen on passing it round. So the game quickly became quite violent, particularly because Clive was still in possession of the wooden mallets. At one point, Daniel tried to intervene and got smacked on the forehead.

The game was interrupted when Boasty Mum 1 started screaming, **'AHHHH! A MOUSE!'**

Sure enough, a small furry body ran out from under a

pile of wrapping paper. Guess who it was?

It was Professor Squeakington!

'It's not a mouse!' I shouted, jumping into the middle of the circle and hunting for him amid the panicked mums and angry babies. Luckily, he wasn't too hard to locate – my heart swelled and I managed to grab him. It was so good to have him safely in my hands again!

'See, he's a hamster,' I said, showing the Boasty Mums.

But they didn't seem convinced.

'You let that thing loose in your house?' said Boasty Mum 2. 'There are babies here! They could get bitten – it's probably diseased!'

How rude!!

'They don't bite . . . much,' I said, trying to remain calm. 'And they are not diseased . . . I don't think. And I didn't let them loose – they escaped earlier. I –'

'They?!' said Boasty Mum 3.

'Yes, this is Professor Squeakington. Fuzzball the Third is still AWOL.'

'What happened to Fuzzball One and Two?' asked Boasty Mum 4.

'It's best not to ask,' replied Toby.

Suddenly Pot Noodle appeared and started running around the living room. He must have somehow managed to break free of his crate.

'POT NOODLE!' I shouted.

'Pot Noodle?!' said Boasty Mum 5, looking really confused.

'Our new dog,' Mum explained.

'You have very strange names for your pets,' she said, raising her eyebrows.

'ORSEY!' shouted Bella with glee, leading the other babies on a rampage, trying to grab poor Pot Noodle's tail.

I started to panic. If he found Fuzzball before me, then

my poor hammy would be a goner!

The next thing I knew, there was a huge clatter from the other side of the living room, where Mum had laid out all the party food. Pot Noodle had jumped on to the table and was busy sticking his nose into EVERYTHING.

'Oh no, not the food!' said Mum.

From Boasty Mum 3 came another shriek: 'Oh my life!!'

But it wasn't the dog running riot on the buffet table that she was looking at. It was Tamara with a big fistful of something . . . brown.

Please say it's chocolate, please say it's chocolate, I prayed as Tamara began smearing the substance all over her face.

EEEEEK!

Reader, it was not chocolate.

Pot Noodle had obvs had another toileting accident without anybody noticing, and now this unlucky baby was trying to eat it.

'POO!' shouted Bella, clapping her hands.

'See, I told you she could say "Poo",' said Toby to the horrified group.

'BUM!' shouted Bella.

'Yep, and "bum".'

Mum looked utterly shell-shocked as she started apologizing profusely and helping Boasty Mum 3 clean up Tamara while instructing Dad to catch Pot Noodle and find the carpet cleaner.

The rest of the BMs started making noises about leaving, which considering the total carnage I can't say I blame them, but poor Mum didn't want them to leave on a bad note. 'You can't go yet,' she said in a panicked voice. 'We've not done the cake! Lottie, could you fetch it and bring it through?'

'Sure,' I said. 'I can do that.'

I took the cake out of the box, grabbed the number '1' candle that Mum had bought and stuck it into the icing, then I lit it with a match.

'Are you ready?' I called out.

'Yes, I think so,' said Dad. 'Come on through.'

I walked down the hall towards the living room as the guests all began to sing 'Happy Birthday' to Bella. Everyone was smiling and singing, so I was relieved to see that the party might end on a high after all.

That was until I got a bit closer. They saw the actual cake and their mouths started hanging open . . .

'That's not . . . That's not the right cake,' said Mum, bringing her hands to her mouth.

I'm not sure anyone believed her as they all started tutting and muttering stuff like, 'What was she thinking?' and 'Very poorly judged!'

It was all very awkward after that, so it wasn't long before the BMs started gathering up their babies and leaving. They said no to offers of taking cake home . . . which was good – more for me!

Bella looked delighted to see the back of them and grabbed a big handful of vodka cake and started stuffing it into her mouth. (Dad quickly had a taste to check it wasn't actually vodka-flavoured, and luckily it was just Victoria sponge.)

3.25 p.m.

Mum called up the cakey-bakey lady and shouted a bunch of stuff down the phone to her along the lines of: 'Yes, I do agree that it was a good cake, but the fact remains that it was **TOTALLY INAPPROPRIATE FOR A FIRST BIRTHDAY!'**

I mean, it was. I absolutely get that, but it did taste nice and I do feel sorry for poor Ben who is eighteen today and got an *In the Night Garden* cake featuring Upsy Daisy flashing her pants at Igglepiggle.

Cakey-bakey lady was very apologetic and started crying down the phone, so Mum said it was fine and accepted a measly £10 refund.

3.33 p.m.

I just found Daniel hiding in the downstairs toilet – he was white as a sheet. I think he's in shock. I'd forgotten he was even here, to be honest. ↘

3.45 p.m.

When I asked Daniel if he was OK, he looked at me as though he couldn't understand what I was saying. I remembered something I'd seen on TikTok about giving sugar to people who've been through a traumatic experience (see, Mum – it's not totally useless!), so I took him into the kitchen and poured him a glass of Coke.

'Drink this,' I told him. 'It's good for the shock.'

After a few mouthfuls, his cheeks got a bit of colour

back and he started to look a bit more alive again.

'What happened?' he asked.

'You came to my house for Bella's birthday, remember?'

'Oh yeh, I think it's coming back to me now . . . Where is everybody?'

'The party is over now, Daniel.'

'Right, yeh, of course. Did they all have a good time?'

'I think so . . .' I said.

Then I gave him a slice of vodka cake and sent him home. Hopefully he's blocked it all out and we'll never have to discuss it again.

5.15 p.m.

Fuzzball the Third has been found! I am sooooooo happy and relieved.

We found him under the buffet table. He was fast

asleep in a piece of discarded wrapping paper, surrounded by half-eaten crudités and cake crumbs – clearly, he'd had the time of his life.

I put him back safely in his cage and I don't think I've ever seen Professor Squeakington so happy.

(8.35 p.m.)

The house is all clean and quiet(ish) again, and Bella and Toby are both asleep.

After everyone had gone, Dad popped to the corner shop and came back with these:

Superhero

KitKat

Sauvignon Blanc

WINE

Not that I'm complaining, but he could have got me more than one considering it had been 14 ENTIRE days since I last ate one!!

I looked at Mum, unsure of what she'd say.

'You've done really well, Laura,' Dad reassured her. 'It's been half a month since you had a glass of wine, and I think you really deserve one today!'

She burst out crying and looked very grateful.

'So . . .' I said, 'have I done really well too? It's also been half a month since I had a KitKat . . .'

They both laughed, and Dad handed me a KitKat.

OMG, it tasted SOOOOOOOOOOOOOOOOOOOOOO good. Mum said exactly the same about her Sauvignon Blanc. Maybe it was worth going cold turkey for a while after all.

Then we snuggled up and watched *The Antiques Roadshow*, which we both enjoy in different ways. Mum likes it when someone takes in something they think is worth hardly anything and it turns out to be worth a hundred grand. I like it when someone takes in something they think is worth a hundred grand and it turns out to be worth a fiver.

Happy place

Anyway, in the middle of a rather boring segment on yet
another antique pocket watch (yawn), Mum turns to me
and says, 'How did that happen, Lottie?'

'What?' I asked.

'Today, I mean. How did it end up being such a mess? I just
wanted to throw a normal party and for the other mums
to accept me. But . . . all the fighting . . . the humping . . .
the poo . . . and the hamsters . . . and the cake – oh God.'
She put her face in her hands. 'Oh dear God, the cake!'

I laughed. I couldn't help myself, because maybe having an extremely embarrassing life runs in the family.

'The problem is,' I told Mum, 'you're trying far too hard to be someone you're not, and those mums will never accept you because unfortunately, just like me, you are a walking recipe for disaster.'

Now it was Mum's turn to laugh. 'Like mother, like daughter, hey?'

'Exactly,' I said, snuggling in for a closer cuddle. 'Now shhhh, because this lady here just said she paid five thousand quid for that terrible vase and I'm pretty sure the presenter guy is about to tell her it's a fake.'

Just in case you're interested – I was right.

MONDAY 16 JANUARY

I think I've upset Jess and Molly.

We saw Daniel on the way to school and he ran up to us. 'Thanks for the great party yesterday. Luckily, the xylophone attack didn't leave a bruise and the vodka cake was delicious.'

I laughed – he'd obviously not blocked it out like I'd hoped, BUT at least he found it funny.

'What party?' asked Molly.

'It was Bella's birthday,' I explained. 'It was . . . eventful.'

Daniel grinned. 'That's one way to describe it.'

'Oh, I didn't know Bella was having a party,' said Jess.

'Me neither,' said Molly. 'I'd have got her a present.'

They both looked a bit upset and then I realized that maybe I should have invited them too. Molly has been

coming to our family parties since we were little, and
Jess adores Bella.

'I've gotta go,' said Daniel, rushing off in the direction
of his form room. 'Give Pot Noodle another tummy rub
from me.'

'He got to meet Pot Noodle as well?' asked Jess, looking
really upset.

'Well . . . yes . . .'

'I thought you said we'd get to meet him first,' said
Molly gloomily.

I felt terrible.

'I'm really sorry, guys,' I said. 'Mum and Dad suggested
inviting Daniel so they could get to know him, but I
should have thought of inviting you too . . . I know how
much you've been wanting to meet the new pup.'

'It's OK.' Jess gave me a little smile. 'I get it.'

'How about you both come over tomorrow and we can take him out for a walk?'

'Cool,' said Molly.

I think we sorted it out, but I still feel guilty – they are my besties after all, and I should really have made sure they were my priority. I'll make it up to them tomorrow.

TUESDAY 17 JANUARY

Molly and Jess came round after school as planned and they absolutely LOVED Pot Noodle.

Mum was a bit nervous about letting me take Pot Noodle out on my own so soon, but we all promised to be super careful and responsible.

The best bit of all was that walking him made us all feel like celebs, because everywhere we went people wanted to stop and pet him and they'd ask us about him. I mean, I guess he is the best-looking dog in the world, right?

We didn't let him off the lead, because Mum said he needs time to bond with us before we can trust him to come back. Pot Noodle didn't seem that bothered though. He was more concerned with wanting to sniff other dogs' private areas – why do they do that?! It's so gross!

After our walk, the girls came back to my house for tea: mac 'n' cheese, which is one of Mum's more palatable dishes. I realized it had been a while since they'd come over for dinner, and I made a promise to myself to not leave it so long next time.

When we'd finished eating, we went to my room and played with the hammies, who have also been feeling a bit rejected lately.

'I'm really sorry you didn't get to meet Pot Noodle first,' I said to Molly and Jess. 'You know I didn't mean to break my promise, right?'

'It's fine,' said Molly, feeding Fuzzball a sunflower seed, 'and of course we know that.'

'Just so long as you don't forget your BFFs come first, *even* if you have a boyfriend!' said Jess, smirking playfully.

I jumped up off the floor and on to my bed, standing up as tall as I could, and made the brownie salute . . .

WEDNESDAY 18 JANUARY

7.33 a.m.

A very bad start to the day. Put my school shoe on and someone had made a nasty deposit inside it.

me, trying not to vom.

Pot Noodle looking very pleased with himself.

I am sick of poo! There is FAR too much of it in this house – it seems as if it's always being cleaned up or talked about, and that's just not how I want to live my life.

It's hard to stay cross with Pot Noodle for long though. He is very lucky that he has such a lovely face.

Dad wrote a note for school, explaining why I was wearing trainers. I threw it in the bin because I'd rather get in trouble than have people find out that my school shoes were full of dog poop. And I know that Mum will say, 'They'll be totally fine after I give them a proper clean,' and I'll have to wear them again tomorrow – gross! IMO they should be incinerated.

(4.35 p.m.)

When I finally got to our form room, I saw Amber talking very excitedly to the group.

'What have I missed?' I asked.

Amber grinned. 'Only the most exciting news of the year!'

'TBF it's only the eighteenth of January, so not much has actually happened yet,' said Molly.

'What is it??' I said, growing impatient.

'The Bad Pancakes have just announced they're playing an extra gig at the Music Hall in a couple of weeks and I'm going to get us all tickets!' Amber told me.

'The Bad Pancakes?!'

Amber gave me a smug look. 'Yes, the band – don't tell me you haven't heard of them, Lottie?!' She took out a flyer from her backpack and put it on the table in front of me.

THE

PANCAKES
4th February
7.30 p.m.
@ Music Hall

'Errrr, well, yeh, obviously I've heard of them!'

FYI, I hadn't. Right now I'm so obsessed with Taylor Swift that I don't have time for anyone else. Especially bands with silly names.

Amber clearly didn't believe me. 'OK, so if you do know them, name one of their songs.'

Why can't she ever let things go? 'Well, I'm not great at remembering song names, but I like the one that goes *BA DA BA DA BA DA DAAAAA BUP BUP BAAAAAA!*'

'Yeh!' said Amber, clapping her hands. 'That one is amazing!'

'Well, maybe they should call themselves the Really Amazing Pancakes then,' I said.

Amber rolled her eyes. 'It's meant to be ironic.'

'Riiiiight. It sounds more like they couldn't think of anything decent to call themselves, so they just used a random band-name generator instead.'

'Whatever, Lottie. If you're going to be like that, then don't come – but me and the girls are all going, right?'

Everyone nodded their heads in agreement. Clearly I was the only one clueless about how un-bad the Bad Pancakes were.

'I didn't say I didn't want to come!' I backtracked.

'Good. Fine. Well, that's sorted then,' said Amber. 'Now we ALL just need to cross our fingers that I get tickets when they go on sale tonight.'

'I've got mine crossed already – I've never been to a proper gig before,' said Jess, sounding super excited.

And that was that. Later during drama, I asked Jess what her favourite Bad Pancakes song was, and she admitted she'd never heard of them either.

5.47 p.m.

I used a band-name generator to help come up with a band name for my future band:

* The Interesting Goldfish Club
* Flight of the Sausages
* Why Spiders, Why?
* Lord of the Amazing Rabbits
* The Super Yummy Pigeons
* King Yellow and the Megafairies
* One Thousand Greasy Pants
* The Shouting Forks Brigade

I thought they were quite good TBH – lots to choose from anyway. Now all I need is a band and some musical talent and I'm well on my way to a Brit Award.

(7.35 p.m.)

TQOEG WhatsApp group:

> **AMBER:** We've got them!!

> **POPPY:** What have you got?! 😕

> **AMBER:** The tickets – duh.

POPPY: Yay!

MOLLY: Double yay!

JESS: Triple yay!

ME: Triple yay and a singular yippee!

AMBER: Annoyingly under-18s need to be supervised by an adult, so my mum or dad are gonna have to come too, but I'll tell them to stay out of our way.

JESS: That's cool. Thanks, Amber.

MOLLY: Thanks for sorting, Amber – I'm so excited! x

POPPY: Cheers, Amber – I can't wait x

ME: Ta, Amber! x

ME: OH, Amber, BTW have you heard of the band The Shouting Forks Brigade?

AMBER: Yeh. I was really into them about two years ago, way before anyone else. They used to be pretty cool, but they are too mainstream now.

HA HA HAAAAAAAAAAAA!

7.45 p.m.

OH MY LIFE, Daniel just messaged . . .

DANIEL: I've got a surprise for you.

ME: What is it???

DANIEL: If I told you, it wouldn't be a surprise, would it?

ME: Well, why are you telling me that you have a surprise for me if you don't want to say what the surprise is?

DANIEL: Good point – do you want me to tell you?

ME: YES!!

DANIEL: OK . . .

ME: Just get on with it!

DANIEL: I got us tickets for the Bad Pancakes gig in two weeks!

My heart dropped.

Daniel was obviously SO excited and it was so kind of him to do this . . . I felt terrible that I was already going.

DANIEL: You still there? Please say you can come! It won't be as fun without you.

ME: Of course I'll come – thank you so much. I can't wait! xx

DANIEL: Brilliant

THOUGHT OF THE DAY:

What did I say that for??? What am I like?!?!

I guess I'll have to tell the girls that I can't go with them. They'll still all have each other, so hopefully they'll understand – fingers crossed anyway!

THURSDAY 19 JANUARY

Met up with Daniel at lunch. We both had pizza slices
and chips and shared a chocolate brownie. He asked
me if I fancied going ice-skating tonight and obvs I said
yes. I hadn't actually been yet this year and I love to
ice-skate (even though I'm not the best at it). I was
really excited, but when I told Jess during double
science she looked a bit . . . I dunno . . . down maybe?

'Are you OK?' I asked her.

At first she kept saying she was fine, but eventually she
explained, 'I guess I just feel a bit sad as the ice rink
will be closing soon and we've not gone together yet.
Sorry, I'm being silly.'

I suddenly remembered last year how me and Jess had
had that fall-out and how we'd finally made up on the
ice rink and skated arm in arm.

'It's not silly,' I told her. 'We've still got time. We'll

sort a date out soon, I promise.'

'Thanks, Lottie. Hey, do you want to get together this weekend and start work on our English project? We've not even agreed on a topic yet and it's only a few weeks away.'

'Deffo! Come round mine and you can hang with Pot Noodle again.'

'Yes! I can't wait to give him some more tummy tickles.'

I grinned, really glad she was smiling again.

Right, I'd better get ready as our session is at five. It's freezing out there tonight so I'm going to wrap up extra-toasty warm.

(7.10 p.m.)

I'm back! Dad dropped me off and I met Daniel by the ticket office – he'd already bought my ticket, which was nice but annoying as he'd paid for the concert tickets too, so it was deffo my turn. We collected our boots (weirdly we are both a size five) and helped each other get them on – why are they always so hard to do up?! Daniel admitted that he'd not been skating for years, so wasn't sure if he was any good or not. That made me feel kind of relieved, because I went last year and so maybe, just maybe, I'd be the better skater of the two of us . . .

And guess what . . . I was right! You should have seen his face when he stepped on the ice: he looked like a rabbit caught in the headlights. And his legs were like a baby deer's – it was hilarious.

At first, Daniel clung to the side for dear life, but eventually I managed to convince him to hold my hand and let go. He was still flailing about all over the place, which made things a lot harder for me, and it wasn't long before we were both in a heap on the ice. Luckily, it didn't put either of us off, and the more we fell over, the funnier it became. I couldn't remember the last time I'd laughed so much, and my stomach was seriously starting to ache.

By the time the whistle went for the end of the session, we'd probably fallen over at least fifteen times. Plus, we were soaking wet and had very sore bottoms. I was looking forward to taking my boots off and getting warm again.

We started skating over to the exit when Daniel grabbed my hand, making me spin round towards him. 'Hey!' I said. 'We've got to get off the ice.'

'I know,' he said with a smile, 'but I just wanted to do this first.' And then he kissed me on the lips in the middle of the rink under the soft pink and purple lights and I'm pretty sure it will remain one of the most romantic moments of my **WHOLE** life.

Dad was waiting for us in the cafe. He handed us hot chocolates and a brownie each and then sat on a different table to give us a bit of privacy. We were very grateful as we were both starving, and they tasted so good!

'The funniest thing,' I told Daniel, who was fidgeting on his seat because of his bruised bum, 'is that it was you who suggested skating in the first place!'

'I know!' He laughed. 'I guess I hoped I'd be a bit better than that, and I thought maybe . . . it would be romantic.'

I smiled. 'I guess it was. In its own way.'

'Let's not do it again anytime soon though – I don't think I'll be able to sit down properly for at least a week.'

Then we both got the giggles again and it didn't help that Dad revealed he'd been taking photos of us from the sidelines. Then passed us his phone to check them out. They made us look like the worst ice-skaters ever – but at least we looked like we were having fun. ☺

THOUGHT OF THE DAY:

I feel so happppppppyyyyyyyyyyyyyyyyyyyyyyyy! I had such a great time tonight. I guess before I had a boyfriend I didn't know what it would be like, but with Daniel it feels like hanging out with Jess, if Jess was a boy. I guess what I mean is that it doesn't feel at all awkward or weird, just comfortable, which for me is a pretty rare thing!

FRIDAY 20 JANUARY

(4.33 p.m.)

I'm home packing my overnight bag with my PJs and toothbrush because today Amber invited us all over for a last-minute sleepover at her house. Only Amber is allowed to do stuff like that – if I asked the Fun Police for a last-minute sleepover with four of my friends, they'd just laugh in my face. Luckily, Amber's family are a lot more chill than mine; in fact, I've barely ever seen them. Amber has so much space and freedom – she's **SO** lucky.

She also said we could get any takeaway we wanted for dinner – it should be really fun! I'm also hoping it will also be the perfect opportunity for me to tell them all that I'm now going to the gig with Daniel. I mean, I'll still see them there and we can hang out together, so I'm really hoping they take it OK and don't get upset.

Just having a quick play with my pup while I'm waiting for Dad to finish work and drop me round Amber's house. I'm really going to miss Pot Noodle and I feel terrible leaving him for the night so soon after he came to live with us.

I take that back – he's humping Teddy One-Eye again!!

Teddy will end up having to have counselling at this rate.

We are currently on Amber's huge bed in our PJs eating a massive Deliveroo order from Nando's and Pho (she has her parents' card details stored in the app). We couldn't agree on which to get, so she said we could just order both – I would NEVER be able to do that at home. When it was delivered, we discovered she had also added loads of drinks, starters and sides and there was **WAY** too much for us to eat. My mum and dad would have gone ballistic, but Amber doesn't seem at all worried about that. Or the fact that there are crumbs and hot sauce all over her bedsheets.

Anyway, I'm just lying here feeling super blissed out and daydreaming about last night . . .

'What are you grinning to yourself about, Lottie?!' said Amber – pretty coldly IMO.

'Nothing,' I replied.

'Then what are you drawing on that piece of paper?'

I looked down and realized that, without even really thinking about it, I'd ripped a page out of Amber's notebook, and I'd been doodling some *slightly* embarrassing stuff on it.

'Don't believe you,' she said, snatching it off me. 'Just as I expected,' she said, holding it up to the group.

'Amber, don't be mean,' said Jess, grabbing the paper and handing it back to me.

I blushed. 'Hey, that's private,' I told her.

'Yeh, well, if it's so private, then why are you doing it at a sleepover when you are meant to be chatting with your *friends*?'

She put an emphasis on the word 'friends' as if she didn't believe I was being a very good one.

Before I had a chance to reply, she carried on, 'I bet you've not even been listening to a word we've been saying, have you?'

Everyone looked at me expectantly.

'I . . . I . . .' I didn't know what to say because – honestly – she was right. I had no idea. I was going to have to make a guess.

'You were talking about . . . whether pineapple on a pizza should be illegal?'

'No.'

'Sloths versus capybaras – which are the cutest?'

'No.'

'How long we'd survive in a zombie apocalypse?'

'No.'

'Taylor Swift's hair?'

'No!'

'OOH, all EXCELLENT topics of convo though, Lotts! I think pineapple –' Poppy started to say.

'See, you weren't listening,' scolded Amber.

I felt kind of bad. 'Sorry, guys,' I said. 'It's just that I really like him . . .'

'We've gathered that based on the fact you are spending ALL your time with him . . .' Amber snapped.

'I'm not spending all my time with him.'

I looked at the others for back-up but didn't get any. Oops.

I tried again. 'I'm here, aren't I?'

'In body, yes,' said Amber, 'but your brain is clearly in Daniel Land.'

'I can't help it.' I grinned. 'We had such a good time yesterday . . .'

I began filling the girls in on our ice-skating date, when Amber started yawning.

'Right, that's it – I'm going to have to get a boyfriend, aren't I?' she said, before taking a bite of her chicken pitta and chewing it thoughtfully.

'Why?' asked Molly.

'Well, it's completely ludicrous that someone like Lottie,' she said, nodding her head in my direction, 'has a boyfriend and I don't.'

'Hmm, good point,' I said, picking up another spring roll.

'It's not a good point,' said Jess, slapping me on the arm. 'That's actually quite insulting!'

'Oh yeh – I mean, bad point.'

'Be quiet, Lottie – no one asked you,' said Amber.

'Well, I think –' I began to say.

'We need to come up with a strategy,' Amber cut in, 'and we need to do it quickly. My reputation is on the line here, and if my reputation is on the line – then so is the reputation of TQOEG.'

We all gasped . . .

'And maybe the rest of you could do with getting boyfriends too,' Amber added. 'It's not a good look, to have so many of us single.'

'EXCUSE YOU!' said Jess, putting her hands on her hips. 'We are STRONG INDEPENDENT WOMEN, and we DO NOT NEED BOYFRIENDS to define ourselves.'

'Speak for yourself, Beyoncé!' huffed Amber.

We all fell about laughing to that, and then we asked Alexa to play 'All the Single Ladies' and spent the rest of the evening recording videos of us doing the dance routine.

Now we are all snuggled up in our sleeping bags, and I'm writing in my diary by the light of my phone. I think everyone else has dropped off already.

(11.58 p.m.)

Tell a lie. Poppy just sat bolt upright and said, 'Sorry, but I don't think I can sleep until I've said this: pineapple on a pizza should be illegal, capybaras deffo win the cute award, we'd survive approximately twenty-seven minutes in a zombie apocalypse because we'd be far too busy scrolling TikTok on our phones, and Tay-Tay's hair looks best medium blonde with a heavy fringe. Goodnight!'

Then she lay back down and closed her eyes and everyone burst out laughing so hard that we all now have tummy aches.

Long live TQOEG – these girls are simply the bestest.

THOUGHT OF THE DAY:

I know what you are wondering: Why didn't Lottie tell the girls about going to the concert with Daniel? Well, I couldn't really, could I? Not when Amber was busy going on about how much I see him at the moment. But I will – I just need to find the right time.

Right, I'm going to sleep now. I'm going to think about Daniel Land and hopefully I'll have a really excellent dream about it, as it sounds like a theme park that I'd really like to go to.

SATURDAY 21 JANUARY

(2.24 p.m.)

We all slept in until after nine. Amber's mum, Melissa,
woke us up by knocking on the door and then leaning
round it.

'Morning, girls!' she said, before tiptoeing into the
room.

She looked dead glamorous. She was wearing smart
jeans with heeled boots, a loose white shirt and a navy
blazer. Her make-up was flawless, complete with bright
red lipstick, and her creamy blonde hair was set into
perfect loose curls – it must have taken her hours to
get ready!

'Morning, Mrs Stevens,' we all said cheerily.

She waved her hand at us dismissively and smiled. 'Oh,
call me Melissa, please. Mrs Stevens makes me sound
like your teacher!'

We all laughed, but Amber looked pretty cross. 'Mum, we were asleep,' she moaned. 'You shouldn't come barging in like that!'

I was quite shocked that she was so rude, especially in front of us. I think we all felt quite awkward.

Melissa pressed her lips together and seemed to give Amber a warning look. 'I'm sorry to wake you up, but I'm about to pop out for coffee with a friend. There's loads to eat for breakfast on the table, so please help yourself.'

'Thank you, Melissa,' we replied. Apart from Amber, who didn't say anything at all.

'That's OK, girls. Stay as long as you like.' She went to close the door, but then popped her head back round. 'Oh and, Amber, don't forget you are going to your dad's today. He's picking you up at two o'clock. Bye, everyone.'

'Bye!'

After she'd closed the door, Poppy turned to Amber. 'What does she mean, you're going to your dad's?'

'Oh, didn't I say?' said Amber, as she picked up a nail file and started filing her nails. 'My mum and dad are getting divorced, so he's moved out.'

We all looked at her in shock.

'What?' said Molly. 'Why didn't you tell us?'

'Not much to tell,' said Amber, sounding bored.

'But . . . are you OK?' I asked.

'I'm fine. In fact, I've never been *more* fine.'

'I'm really sorry to hear that, Amber,' said Jess.

'Me too,' said Poppy. 'It must be difficult –'

'It's actually really great,' interrupted Amber. 'It means twice the amount of clothes, holidays, birthday presents *and* pocket money. They feel really guilty, so they're basically buying me whatever I want!'

She grinned as she said it and looked happy, but I don't think any of us were convinced. I mean, does she even need more stuff?! She has almost everything a teenager could possibly want.

'If you ever want to talk about it, you know –' started Molly.

'I won't,' said Amber, jumping up. 'Right, let's get breakfast. I'm starving.'

We went downstairs to see what Melissa had left us for breakfast, but Amber looked unimpressed with the vast array of muffins, cereals, croissants, fruit and juices on the breakfast bar.

We all tried to reassure her if was more than enough. It looked like something you'd get at a hotel, but she insisted on making another Deliveroo order for French toast, cream, berries, bacon, maple syrup and pancakes anyway. Even though it seemed completely unnecessary, it was yum, yum and more yum.

The Beyoncé sesh last night clearly didn't have much impact on her, as she was still banging on about getting a boyfriend.

'Right, I've got it,' I said, loading up another pancake with cream and strawberries. 'You could advertise the position and conduct interviews with the most eligible bachelors.'

I was joking (obvs), but that must have gone right over Amber's head, because she clapped her hands and said, 'YES! Lottie – you must have some brain cells after all.'

'Errr, I think that was another insult,' said Jess.

'Shhhhh, Jess – no one cares. OK, let's start with designing the application form. Poppy, you can be the notetaker.'

'Can I finish my food first, please, boss?' Poppy asked, stabbing another rasher of crispy bacon with her fork.

Amber sighed. 'What's more important, Poppy? Bacon or me getting a boyfriend?'

'Is this a trick question?' she asked.

Amber gave her a death stare and Poppy promptly put the bacon back on the plate. It never fails to surprise me just how much authority Amber seems to have over people.

She got her laptop and instructed us that we needed to get to work immediately. I looked forlornly at the remaining pancakes as we headed upstairs.

An hour later, we were done – or, rather, Poppy had finished typing up Amber's strict demands. I had to admit though, it looked pretty good . . .

Application for the position of Amber's Boyfriend

Name:

Phone number:

DOB: (Minimum age 13)

Hair colour:

Eye colour:

Height: (Minimum 5'4")

Number of social media followers:

How much disposable income do you have?

Do you have any bad habits? If so, what are they?

What do you like most about Amber?

Why would you make a good boyfriend?

Where would you take Amber on your first date?

Rate yourself out of 10 for the following attributes:

Looks:

Intelligence:

Popularity:

I do solemnly and sincerely and truly declare and affirm that the evidence I have given is the truth, the whole truth and nothing but the truth.

Signed: _____

Date: _____

Amber read the application form back out to the group. 'It's perfect, don't you think?'

Jess raised her eyebrows. 'If shallow is what you were aiming for, then it's perfect, yeh.'

Amber looked surprised. 'Really?!'

Ever the diplomat, Molly tried to explain. 'I think what Jess means is that it's a bit materialistic. It doesn't really ask too much about the applicants' . . . personality.'

'Personality?' mused Amber, as if it was a totally new concept.

'Yeh, you know, what sort of person they are, what hobbies they have, what they find funny . . .' I added.

'Exactly,' said Molly. 'At the moment, the application questions focus mainly on looks, popularity and how much money they have – but what if you don't have anything in common?'

'I think you guys are completely missing the point,' Amber scoffed. 'If they are good-looking, popular and have lots of money, then we will have LOADS in common.'

Jess rolled her eyes. 'True dat.'

Amber smiled. 'Thanks, Jess.' Once again, she had completely missed the sarcasm. Then she eyed Jess suspiciously. 'Now, what about you?'

'Huh? What about me?' asked Jess, looking confused.

'Well, what are you going to do about getting a boyfriend? I mean . . . since I met you, you've never even talked about a guy you like. Do you have a crush on anyone?'

'I, um . . . I –'

'Because if you did, then maybe I could help set you up with him,' Amber said eagerly. 'I LOVE a project! There must be someone you like . . .'

'Amber, leave Jess alone,' I said. 'She doesn't have to –'

Jess put her hand on my shoulder. 'It's OK, Lottie,' she said nervously. 'No, Amber, there isn't anyone I like, and that's because . . . I don't know if I even like –' she took a deep breath – 'boys . . . like that, I mean.'

We all looked at her, only me really understanding the significance of what she was saying.

'What do you mean?' asked Poppy, frowning.

'I mean . . .' said Jess in a quiet, shaky voice, 'that I think I might be . . . gay.'

For a few seconds the room was dead silent. No one quite knew how to react.

Then the squealing began . . .

Amber declared, 'This is the best news ever – I've always wanted a gay bestie!'

'Amber!' I said. 'You can't say that.'

Jess laughed and said, 'It's OK!' I think she was just relieved everyone was reacting so well. Not that there was any doubt in my mind that the group would be anything other than supportive.

'I'm so glad you told us,' said Molly. 'It was really brave.'

'I mean, I was pretty nervous.' Jess smiled at the four of us. 'I've been trying to find the right moment.'

'So, how long have you known? Are there any girls you like? Have you told anyone else?' asked Poppy excitedly.

'Hey, chill with all the questions!' I said.

Jess laughed again. 'I've known a while, but it all feels quite new still . . . No, there's no one I like, and only my mum knows . . . and Lottie,' she added, smiling at me.

I smiled back at her, feeling special that she'd confided in me first.

Later, when we'd gathered up our stuff, Poppy asked if we wanted a lift home with her dad. Molly said yes, but I was glad when Jess said she'd prefer to walk, because I wanted a chance to talk to her on my own.

'I didn't know you were going to do that today,' I said.

'Neither did I,' she said, 'but then I thought, *Why not?* I mean, sometimes it's best to blurt it out, right? If I'd have planned it, then maybe I'd have bottled it.'

'I guess,' I replied.

We fell silent for a minute; we were nearly back at hers. When we reached her gate, I finally said what I'd been wanting to tell her: 'I'm really proud of you, Jess.'

'Thanks, Lottie. That means a lot. It really does.'

Then we hugged and waved each other goodbye.

When I got home, I told Mum about Jess being gay and she was very impressed with how Jess had handled it and how supportive we all were of her. Apparently, when she was at high school, no one was openly gay, for fear of getting bullied. It made me feel sad, but also very relieved that Jess wouldn't have to go through that – TQOEG were going to be beside her every step of the way.

4.12 p.m.

Just got off the phone with Poppy. She called to chat about Amber. After Jess's big news, I'd almost forgotten about Amber's parents' divorce!

'She seems surprisingly OK though, doesn't she?' I said.

'I dunno,' said Poppy, sounding quite unsure. 'She often puts on an act – it's difficult to know how she's really feeling.'

I thought about how Amber had been a bit moodier than usual lately, and about a few of the mean comments she had made. Was it because she was hurting inside? Perhaps it was why she suddenly wanted to get a boyfriend too. Maybe it was a distraction, or maybe she was just feeling lonely?

'What do you think we should do?' I asked Poppy.

She sighed. 'Just be there for her and try to be a bit more understanding, I guess. Despite what she says, I'm sure it can't be easy.'

I thought of my parents and how I'd feel if they split up. 'No, it can't be easy at all.'

SUNDAY 22 JANUARY

SO TIRED!

Pot Noodle was crying to be let out for a wee and apparently it's my duty to help out with that at the weekends. I was still tired from the sleepover and I really didn't want to get out of bed – it was freezing! The Fun Police would be super annoyed if they had to get up though, so I counted to three, pushed my covers aside and quickly grabbed my dressing gown. Then I slowly made my way downstairs, looking and feeling like the undead.

Pot Noodle, unlike me, was bouncing about in his crate like a pinball. When I let him out, he jumped up and licked me all over my face, so I couldn't stay cross at him for long – although I was quite alarmed by how awake he seemed at silly o'clock in the morning.

I let him out into the garden to do his business, but he seemed way more interested in running around, sniffing and barking at the moon.

'SHHHHHH, Pot Noodle,' I told him. 'People are sleeping.'

Unfortunately, he didn't care that people were still asleep. Instead, he found his ball and ran over to me and dropped it by my feet.

'It's night-time. I'm not playing ball with you, you crazy puppy!' I said, scolding him. 'Can you just go to the toilet like a good dog and then we can both go back to bed?'

Reader, he would not listen to me! He simply wagged his tail, ran round in circles and refused to go to the toilet, leaving me standing there in my dressing gown and freezing my little butt off – and did I mention that it had also started to rain?

After about ten minutes, it became clear that the negotiations were not going well, so I gave up. I managed to grab Pot Noodle and put him back in his crate, then I wished him goodnight, but PN started crying each time I tried to leave him. In the end I decided the best thing for it was to take him into the living room and make a bed for myself on the sofa, and we could both get some more sleep.

So here we are now: the electric blanket is on, I've put on a *Friends* episode on the TV, PN is snuggled up next to me and I'm about to take a nice little nap (as soon as I've finished my early morning Cheerios). Hopefully Mum will be very grateful to me when she wakes up.

7.44 a.m.

Mum was not very grateful. In fact, she wasn't grateful one bit.

I was rudely awakened by her shouting, **'OH MY GOD! OH MY GOD! LOTTIE, WHAT ON EARTH?'**

At first, I was very confused, because I was having a

dream that I was on a spaceship about to take off on a
mission to establish a settlement on the moon.

Slowly I adjusted back to reality and it turns out that
while I was dozing, Pot Noodle had been having a fun
time in the living room. And by 'a fun time', I mean he
had been destroying everything in sight.

He had ripped up cushions, upended a plant pot,
knocked my breakfast bowl over, chewed two of the
legs of the coffee table – oh, and he'd also trodden mud
all over the sofa and carpet.

I was actually quite impressed with the amount of
naughty behaviour he had squeezed into the past hour
TBH.

'I'm sorry, Mum,' I said sheepishly. 'We were both
asleep on the sofa and –'

'If you weren't supervising him properly, then he
should have been in his crate!' Mum said crossly.

Pot Noodle trotted off to pick up something from
the corner of the room and brought it over to Mum,
looking very pleased with himself.

'Oh no, not my favourite bra!' she cried.

'You have a favourite bra?!' I said.

'Well, I did, and now it's totally mangled,' she said,
looking utterly devastated. 'It's not easy finding bras
that fit well when you're in your forties . . . I've had this
one for nearly ten years.'

'Ewwww, that's gross,' I said.

'That is not the point, Lottie. Look at this mess – I want you to clean it all up immediately and this,' she said, holding up a horrible, grey, ugly bra, 'is coming out of your pocket money!'

I mean, if she's taking any more than 50p, then I'll be fuming! Right, I suppose I'd better get on.

(11.52 a.m.)

Took me AGES to clean up Pot Noodle's mess! I was so tired afterwards I had another little nap and was woken up by Jess calling. She wanted to know what time she should come round to work on our English project. **EEK** – I had completely forgotten!

Even though I knew we really needed to get started on it, I was feeling SO tired that I managed to convince her that we should do it one evening next week instead. She was OK about it (I think) – it's just that she's quite geeky with schoolwork and always wants to do her best. That is great, usually, as it means when I work with her I get good marks, but today not so much be-cause I'm so, so, sooooooo tired and I don't think I can get myself up off the sofa.

Got myself into a liiiiiiitle bit of a situation and I cannot decide if I was being unreasonable or not?!

Maybe you can help me decide . . .

Even though I was absolutely exhausted, the Fun Police dragged me out on a family dog walk because of the whole 'being a responsible dog owner' thing, blah blah blah.

We ended up playing fetch, which was fun for a bit . . . and then less fun because Pot Noodle seemed to prefer catching any ball but ours and it became mega awks when he refused to give the balls back to their owners.

After an hour or so, we were about to head home, when I spotted Daniel and Theo having a kickabout.

'Hey, guys,' I called out, walking towards them.

Daniel spotted me and grinned. 'Hi, Lottie.'

'Hiya,' said Theo.

'Give me five minutes, mate,' Daniel said to Theo, before running over.

'What you doing?' he asked me.

'Just been walking the dog with the fam,' I replied. 'Heading home now though – I'm frozen.'

He put his arm round me and I suddenly felt all warm inside. 'Naaaa, don't go!' he said. 'We should hang for a bit – fancy going on the swings?'

I was like, 'DO I EVER?!' I'd not been on a swing for ages.

'What about Theo though?' I asked.

'He won't mind,' said Daniel.

'HEY, MATE!' he shouted over to Theo, who was playing keepy-uppies. 'I'm off to the swings with Lottie – see ya later!'

Theo held out his arms as if to say, *What?!* Then he hoofed the ball halfway across the park and walked off, looking pretty cross.

'Maybe you should have stayed,' I said to Daniel.

'Nah, we've been here ages – he'll be OK.'

I said goodbye to Mum and Dad, and we went over to the swings. Luckily there were two free next to each other. We started swinging away, laughing, joking and playing a game of who can go the highest (he thought he did, but it was deffo me). I felt like a little kid and a grown-up all at once. Then I spotted Jess spinning her little sis, Florence, on the roundabout. And it occurred to me that if Jess saw me out with Daniel, then she might be a teeeeeny-weeeeeny bit cross that I said I was too tired to work on our project together.

WHOOPS.

Before I had a chance to think about it any further – i.e. hide – Florence had spotted me.

'OTTTIIIIIEEE! IZ OTTIIIIIEEE!' she shrieked happily, pointing at me and jumping up and down.

I stopped my swing and hopped off, then Flo came running over and jumped right into my arms. She's such a cutie – I'd definitely swap her for Bella if Mum would let me.

'I go roundy roundy roundy!' she told me, giggling.

I laughed. 'Did you get dizzy?'

'Yes!' she squealed, and started spinning round in circles.

'Hi, Lottie,' said Jess, appearing behind her.

I could tell she wasn't happy with me, by the tone of her voice. Not that it was cross-sounding; it was just not very happy, friendly Jess-sounding.

'Hi, Jess,' said Daniel, 'and hi, Jess's little sister. Would you like me to push you on the swings?'

'YES!!' screamed Florence, clapping her hands.

Then it was just me and Jess, and neither of us knew quite what to say.

'It's not how it –' I started to explain.

'You didn't look very tired, up there on the swings,' she interrupted.

'I know, but I was earlier. I'd just woken up when you called, but then –'

'If you'd rather spend time with him than me, then at least be honest about it.'

OUCH.

'It's not that! Mum and Dad dragged me out for a walk, and I was about to go home but then I saw Daniel . . . It wasn't planned, I swear.'

She looked at me, frowning, clearly trying to work it all out in her head.

'Jess, I'm sorry,' I continued. 'I can see how this looks, and I feel terrible, but I wasn't even going to come out . . .'

'Really?'

'Yes, I promise. I shouldn't have bailed on you though. I wish I hadn't.'

'Yeh, you shouldn't have,' she replied, but there was a little smile trying to break through on her face. Then she starting wagging her finger at me. 'This is NOT BFF behaviour, you know, Lottie!'

'I know – what can I do to make it up to you?'

'Well, let's see . . . You could take over as chief roundabout pusher for starters. My arms are killing me and she loves that blummin' thing!

'Deal!'

As it actually turned out, Florence wanted Daniel to take over as roundabout pusher and for me to ride on

it with her. I think I got the worse deal by far, because I'd forgotten how badly they give me motion sickness.

I felt hideous when we were finally allowed off by the boss, and I nearly vommed in a bush.

(7.22 p.m.)

I know me and Jess sorted stuff out, but I was still feeling super guilty about earlier. It's really unusual for her to be angry with me, so when she is, I know I crossed a line.

Decided to WhatsApp her to triple-check everything was cool between us.

ME: Hey, bestie, I'm so sorry about earlier. It was selfish of me. Hope we are OK? Xx

JESS: Of course we are cool! I'm sorry too if I was a bit snappy. I guess I'm just feeling nervous about tomorrow . . .

ME: Tomorrow? Why? What's happening?

JESS: Well, I'm kind of guessing that now it's out in the open, people at school will start to find out I'm gay . . .

ME: Oh! Of course. But you told us and we were all super supportive, so I'm sure everyone else will be!

JESS: Yes, but it's quite different telling you guys vs loads of randoms. I'm scared. What if people are mean? Or don't want to hang out with me any more?

ME: No one is going to be mean and why would anyone NOT want to hang out with you?! Plus, if anyone does have a problem with it, then they will have me and the rest of TQOEG to deal with!! We can be very scary when we want to be, you know! 😣

JESS: 🤣 You da best, Lottie x

ME: No, YOU da best x

JESS: No, YOU da best x

ME: No, YOU da best x

ETC. ETC.

THOUGHT OF THE DAY 1:
Gotta up my BFF game – Jess needs me right now! And possibly Amber too . . . On Friday, everything was pretty normal and now they are both going through some pretty life-changing stuff.

Man, it's a busy life managing my friends, my boyfriend, my family, my pup, my schoolwork AND my eyebrows.

THOUGHT OF THE DAY 2:
I hope I never get so old and boring that I have a favourite bra!

MONDAY 23 JANUARY

When Jess said she guessed people might find out she was gay today . . . she was NOT wrong.

News sure travels fast in Kingswood High (with help from Amber's big mouth). I don't think Jess minded though – it just meant she didn't have to go around telling people herself.

'Feeling better about everything today?' I asked her at lunch.

'Much!' she said. 'I feel like a weight has been lifted off my shoulders.'

'And no one's said anything mean?'

'Well, when I walked into the canteen with Molly, one of the TUMGG – I think it was Candice – shouted out, "Here come the lesbians!"'

I scowled. 'How's that funny?!'

'It's not,' said Molly. 'I shouted back, "*Takes one to know one!*"'

'And everyone laughed – *at* them, not *with* them,' said Jess, putting an arm round Molly.

'That's great,' I said, smiling. 'Well done, Molly.'

Then Jess explained that she's also decided to join the LGBTQ+ club that school runs on Wednesday lunchtimes, which is cool, and super brave. I said I'd go with her for moral support, which she was really pleased about. I'm glad that our (kind of) fight yesterday has been forgotten – phew.

The other news is that Amber brought her stack of applications into school, and she made us all take a pile each and hand them out at lunchtime.

'Please pay attention to the minimum age and height requirements before you hand one out,' she called. 'I don't want you to waste your time, or more importantly . . . mine.'

She also told us to pay particular attention to the Year

Nine boys, most of whom seemed to find the situation highly amusing. Me and Jess got a bit bored and started giving them out to anyone we could, then Amber had to run after a bunch of tiny Year Sevens and snatch them back. Her self-confidence levels are incredibly impressive!

Finally, Amber placed a postbox she had made in our form room, for boys to submit their completed applications. Mr Peters eyed it suspiciously and she simply told him, 'It's part of a personal development project, sir.'

He seemed quite distracted, so he just muttered, 'Oh right, well, great work, Amber,' and she got two good behaviour points!

Great work?! Am I living on a totally different planet to everyone else?!

URGH. Anyway, Amber has set the application deadline for Friday, and then she'll be shortlisting the candidates. And, yes, she did use the word 'candidates'!

PS Since the weekend, Amber hasn't said anything else about her parents' divorce. Poppy and Molly both tried to speak to her about it again, but she just changed the subject and insisted she wasn't bothered. Maybe she is totally fine? It's hard to say, but we've all agreed to keep an eye on her and be there for her whenever she needs.

TUESDAY 24 JANUARY

Daniel asked me if I wanted to meet up after school tomorrow and go for a hot chocolate or something. I said yes (obvs), but when I was telling the girls about it over lunch, Amber kept fake yawning and changing the subject.

I tried to ignore her, but then she goes, 'You know what, Lottie? You've got dead boring since you got a boyfriend – all you do is talk about him, like it's the ONLY topic of conversation you can think of.'

'That's not true!' I said.

'Yes, it is. We've been on our lunch break for –' she looked at her watch – 'twenty-two minutes now and it's been *Daniel, Daniel, Daniel, blah blah blah.*'

I looked around the table at the other girls to back me up, but they were all laughing.

Amber, clearly spurred on by the reaction she was getting, put on a high-pitched voice and started doing an impression of me . . .

That made everyone crease up, even Jess. I was getting really cross with Amber – why did she have to make fun of me?!

Molly looked at me and said, 'Oh come on, Lottie. She's only messing about – she doesn't mean it.'

'But it's not even true – I don't talk about Daniel *all* the time.'

I looked at Jess and Poppy for support.

Poppy giggled and said, 'Ummm, you kind of do.'

'But we don't mind . . .' Jess added quickly. 'We're happy for you!'

I can't lie – it hurt. I'd obviously been doing it more than I thought, so what else could I do but back down and change the subject. 'Fine. I'm sorry. Would anyone like a Monster Munch?'

I regretted saying that as soon as it had come out of my mouth, as obviously everyone did, so I only got three to myself. Still, at least it won me a few brownie points back.

I pretended everything was cool after that, but I was actually quite annoyed. I mean, maybe I have been talking about Daniel a bit too much lately, but why does Amber have to make a big deal out of it and do that silly impression?! I doubt anyone else would have even noticed if it wasn't for her, but now she's planted the seed, I'm going to worry about mentioning his name ever again.

When I got home, I was still feeling quite confused

about everything and then I remembered Felicity the fortune-telling fish! I got her out of my desk drawer, placed her in my hand and I asked her what the deal was with Amber.

She moved her head, so I looked up what that meant . . .

WEDNESDAY 25 JANUARY

Woke up feeling good today. I had a date with Daniel after school and I was really looking forward to it. I just wasn't going to talk about it (much).

The feeling didn't last too long though, because when I got to registration all the other girls were already there and Amber goes, 'Lottie, hey. We're all gonna go to Costa later. The hot chocolates are on me – wanna come?'

'Can't,' I said, frowning. 'I'm getting hot chocolate with Daniel, remember?'

'Well, if you'd rather get hot chocolate with your boyfriend than your friends, then that's up to you.'

I was dead confused. She knew I couldn't come – I'd told them all yesterday I was hanging out with Daniel.

'I wouldn't,' I said crossly. 'I just can't today, that's all.'

'WOW, somebody's in a bad mood. Did you get your period, Lottie?' smirked Amber.

I tried not to let it get to me – it's not like I could object to the girls doing something without me, but why couldn't they have picked Thursday or Friday instead? It almost felt as though Amber was trying to purposely exclude me.

I kept my distance from the gang for the rest of the day, mostly to avoid Amber. I ate my lunch with Daniel and I didn't even see the girls in the canteen, so maybe they were trying to avoid me too.

After lunch, I saw Jess by the lockers and tried to talk to her about Amber and how she was making me feel, but she didn't even seem to care. She was really quiet, and when I asked her what was wrong, she said, 'Not everything is always about you, you know, Lottie!'

I bit my lip, as I felt a bit like I might cry.

So now even Jess was mad at me?! What have I done – I just don't get it!!

I was really glad when the final bell rang and I found Daniel waiting for me outside maths, with a big smile.

'Where do you want to go?' he asked.

I didn't want to bump into the girls, so I suggested Starbucks and we walked there hand in hand, talking about our days. I didn't tell him anything about the Amber situation, because I wanted to forget about it and enjoy myself, but as soon as we sat down with our drinks, Amber, Molly, Poppy and Jess burst through the doors, laughing and giggling.

When they saw us, they came over to say hi.

'I thought you were going to Costa,' I said.

'It was rammed,' said Molly, 'so Amber suggested coming here.'

'If I'd have known you'd have been here, obviously we'd have tried somewhere else,' said Amber, smiling. 'Sorry to crash your *romantic* date. Come on, girls – let's leave these two lovebirds to it.'

God, why does she make everything so awks??

'Bye, Lottie,' said Molly.

'Have fun,' said Poppy.

Jess didn't say a thing!

They went off to order and then sat a few tables away from us, so it was almost impossible to chat to Daniel without getting distracted, especially when they were laughing and giggling so loudly.

'Do you want to leave?' asked Daniel, obviously sensing I was feeling uneasy.

'Yeh, I've finished – you?'

'Yep.'

Then he walked me back home and came inside to give Pot Noodle a tummy tickle. It was nice for him to see the family again (under more normal conditions) and for once everyone was behaving themselves – even Toby! In fact, Daniel was really great with him. He went over to Toby, who was on the iPad playing *Minecraft*, and asked him what he was building. I tried to warn Daniel that getting into a *Minecraft* convo with Toby was probably a bad idea as it can go on FOREVER, but he said he didn't mind. He told Toby that he used to play *Minecraft* loads when he was younger, and he gave Toby a bunch of tips that he was super chuffed about.

When he left, the whole family told me how much they liked Daniel.☺

THURSDAY 26 JANUARY

7.55 a.m.

Going to focus on the positives today: things with Daniel are good and I'm going to stop letting myself feel left out by the gang. I'm going to be my usual cheerful self and not let anything get me down. Plus, Jess is coming over after school so we can finally get to work on our English assignment – we are really behind now, so we have LOTS to do! It will be great to hang out with her, one on one, as it feels like it's been ages since it's been just us two.

6.45 p.m.

Despite what I said this morning, I did let things get to me.

Things with TQOEG were fine(ish), except that they were talking a lot about how funny it was at Starbucks yesterday. Apparently Amber did a really funny impression of Mr Peters, and Molly laughed so much that her Frappuccino came out of her nose, which made Poppy laugh so hard she started snorting her Frappuccino, and before long all four of them were snorting Frappuccinos left, right and centre. Supposedly it was hilarious, but it just sounds like a complete waste of good Frappuccinos to me!

Jess was still being pretty distant though, with me at least. I mean, she answered questions and stuff, but she wasn't her usual self. I was really confused and looking forward to chatting to her later when I had her on her own.

After school, I met her by the gates and although she smiled and said hi, she was noticeably quiet as we started to walk home. I couldn't work it out, but I knew I had to find out if anything was wrong.

When we got back to my house, I just blurted it out. 'Jess, have I done something to upset you?'

She sighed. 'Sometimes, I just feel like I'm not that important to you any more.'

'What? Of course you are – you're my BEST friend. What do you mean?'

'Nothing. It doesn't matter.'

'It does matter. I want to fix this – please tell me what I've done!'

She turned to look at me and I noticed she had tears in her eyes . . .

OMG.

I'd totally forgotten. What an idiot!

Tears started to roll down her face. 'You said you'd come with me, and you weren't there.'

'I just . . . I . . .' I could barely even speak. What was I even meant to say to make this any better?

'And you've not even asked me a single thing about it . . .'

'I'm so sorry. I know it's a terrible excuse, but I completely forgot.'

'Amber says that you've got your priorities all wrong.'

That annoyed me. What was Amber doing, stomping in with her size six DMs? 'What's this got to do with her?'

'Well, at least she came with me to the group and supported me. Now you've got a boyfriend, I barely see you!'

I felt absolutely terrible.

'I'm really, REALLY sorry, Jess. I've been distracted lately, I know that. But I want to make it right, please believe me.'

She didn't say anything, but I could tell she was turning things over in her head.

I put my arms round her. 'You are my bestest-ever BFF and nothing, and no boy, is going to change that – OK?'

'You swear?' she asked with a small smile.

'On my hammies' lives!' I said.

'Lottie, you can't say that!!!'

'Sorry, guys, I'm only joking,' I called out to my hamsters.

'Phew, I should hope so too,' Jess said, laughing.

'So, tell me everything about yesterday,' I said. 'Did you meet anyone nice?'

'Yes, they were all really nice.'

'But was there anyone *nice* nice?'

Jess blushed. 'I met a really cool person called Cleo.'

This was *interesting*. 'Is she in our year?'

'Yes, but Cleo's non-binary, so they use the pronouns "they" and "them".'

'Well, I'd like to meet them one day.'

'Maybe you will, but for now we've got to get on with this project. I watched a nature documentary on bumblebees the other day. Did you know that they are seriously endangered?'

'No way,' I said sadly. 'I love bees!'

'Me too – so what do you think about doing our project on that?'

'It's a great idea.' I grinned. 'Let's get our geek on and get to work!'

THOUGHT OF THE DAY:

I'm so glad I worked things out with Jess, but why is Amber talking about me behind my back?

I know she's going through a difficult time at home and maybe I'm feeling paranoid, but sometimes it feels as though she's taking all her anger out on me. I really thought she'd changed, but it's not the first time she's tried to come between me and Jess.

FRIDAY 27 JANUARY

Amber messaged us all to get to school early. As usual, everyone complied.

She took the applications out of the postbox. 'Right,' she said, leafing through them. 'We have a total of . . . hmm . . . twenty-two, twenty-three, twenty-four, *twenty-five!*'

'Wow!' said Poppy.

'It's not bad,' said Amber, 'but I expected a few more.'

She expected a few more?!

'OK, now we need to whittle them down, so we can interview the most promising boys.'

I was SHOOK. 'You're going to interview them?!'

'Yes, Lottie. Keep up – how else would I find the best person for the job?'

'I think I missed the part where having a boyfriend was an actual job,' I said. 'I didn't realize you were going to pay them.'

'Of course I'm not going to pay them, Lottie – if anything, they should be paying *me*!'

The rest of the girls burst out laughing at this point and Amber gave them icy stares. 'Is something funny?'

She waited until the giggles had stopped and then said, 'Right, Poppy, you can go through these tonight and shortlist them. Get rid of anyone too short, young, immature or just . . . weird. Then WhatsApp the finalists, congratulating them on making the finals and invite them for a formal interview on Monday in the Eight-G form room.'

I waited for Poppy to say no, but she took the stack of papers without saying a word.

'Could you not do it yourself?' I asked Amber.

'I'm pretty busy, in case you haven't noticed, Lottie. People to see, things to do!'

I rolled my eyes. It's unbelievable what Amber gets away with.

After school, we went to Frydays and talked about what we were doing over the weekend. No one made any plans to meet up, so when Daniel came over and asked if I wanted to go to his house for lunch, I said yes.

'Is that OK?' I asked Jess after he'd gone.

She smiled. 'Course it is.'

THOUGHT OF THE DAY:
Excited about seeing Daniel tomorrow.
But I just realized that that also means I
have to . . .

SATURDAY 28 JANUARY

Just woke up from a horrible dream!

I went round to Daniel's house, which turned out to be a really spooky castle in Transylvania (not quite sure how we got there as I don't remember flying). I rang the bell and Count Dracula answered and it turned out that he was Daniel's dad! Then I met Daniel's mum, who was a lady vampire, and they asked me to come through to the dining room for dinner. Long story short: it turned out that the dinner was me and they wanted to suck my blood!

I've no idea where Daniel was the whole time, but I remember thinking it was rather rude to invite your girlfriend round to meet your parents and then just go AWOL while they killed her.

Luckily it was just a dream, phew. I do keep having quite bizarre dreams at the minute though – maybe it's because I eat too much cheese?!

10.09 a.m.

What on earth do people wear when they meet the parents for the first time? Should I go in my regular everyday clothes, or should I dress up a bit? When I saw Daniel's parents at the school performance of *The Little Mermaid* last year they looked kind of posh – or maybe posher than my family anyway (but that's not hard).

I was dressed as a crab back then. Should I dress up as a crab again today??

No, Lottie – of course you shouldn't dress up as a crab **FGS!**

I'll have to have a rifle through the wardrobe. BRB.

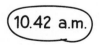

10.42 a.m.

So I'm down to four looks . . .

Please can you vote for your fave?

1. Regular Lottie   2. Crab Lottie   3. Geek Lottie   4. Count Lottie

OK, the votes are in, and it was a close call (well, I only asked Pot Noodle and the hammies) and the result is . . .

OUTFIT THREE!!

5.23 p.m.

Knocked on Daniel's door and he opened it and was like, 'What on earth are you wearing?'

267

'Charming!' I said.

'Since when do you wear glasses?'

I looked at my watch. 'Since about thirty-eight minutes ago.'

He showed me in and I tripped over the doorstep (on account of not being able to see properly).

'Can you even see properly in those things?' asked Daniel.

'See properly? Of course I can see properly! I wouldn't be wearing glasses that made me see worse, would I? How silly do you think I am?' I replied, nearly tripping over again.

He gave me a funny look and took me through to the kitchen, where his mum and dad were sitting at the table drinking some tea (I was glad to see it wasn't blood TBH).

'Lottie,' said Daniel's mum, standing up and coming over to greet me. She gave me a big smile (no fangs, phew!) and said, 'How are you? It's lovely to finally meet you.'

I put on what I thought was a posh voice: 'I'm

gooooooooood. It's lovely to meet yoooooou tooooooo.'

Daniel opened his eyes wide and nudged me. 'Why are you talking like an owl?' he whispered.

I shrugged. It was just what came out – how was I supposed to know why I was doing it?!

His mum gave me an odd look and said, 'Call me Kate, please, and this is Tony,' she added, gesturing at Daniel's dad.

Tony put his paper down and held his hand out to shake mine. 'Nice to meet you, Lottie.'

'Twiiit twooooooo, Tooooony,' I said.

OMG, that was Daniel's fault for putting owl vibes into my head when I was already nervous!!

I reached my hand out towards Tony's, but I ended up shaking some air instead. 'These are new glasses,' I explained. 'I think maybe they got the prescription wrong.'

Everyone laughed nervously.

Kate asked if I wanted some tea, and even though I hate tea, I said yes. Then when she asked what tea I'd like, I said Earl Grey as it sounded fancy?! Once the tea was made (it was very disgusting), we all sat down at the table and they asked me some questions about school and my family. I think I answered them in a relatively normal way. I mean, I may have started rambling on a bit and maybe I blurted out a few random thoughts, but at least there weren't any awkward silences.

After a while Tony and Kate said they'd 'better dash', and I took the glasses off and tipped the tea into the sink as soon as they left the kitchen – phew.

'How do you think it went?' I asked Daniel.

'I mean . . . fine, apart from the fact that you were wearing glasses you clearly couldn't see out of and the whole talking-like-an-owl thing.'

'You should be glad I didn't turn up dressed like a vampire,' I told him.

Daniel gave me a very strange look and laughed. 'You never fail to surprise me, Lottie Brooks,' he said.

I grinned. 'What shall we do now?' I asked.

'We're going to make lunch,' he told me.

'You invited me round to lunch and I have to make it myself?!'

'Basically, yes,' said Daniel, taking my hand and leading me to the kitchen counter. 'Welcome to Daniel's Pizzeria!' he announced.

My eyes widened. There were two big blobs of pizza dough, a little tub of flour, a big pot of tomato sauce and bowls of just about every pizza topping you could imagine – ham, bacon, pepperoni, grated cheese, sliced mozzarella, pineapple, peppers, sweetcorn, mushrooms, olives and jalapenos!

'This is brilliant!' I said, laughing. 'What do we do first?'

'We roll the dough,' said Daniel, taking a pinch of flour and throwing it up into the air like a cloud of smoke.

We had such a fun time making our pizzas and pretending we were Italian chefs on a TV show. I made mine with pepperoni, bacon, sweetcorn and LOADS of cheese, and I swear it was the best pizza I had ever tasted. Daniel had ham, mushroom, peppers and olives, and he said the exact same thing.

'I'd rate Daniel's Pizzeria four and a half out of five,' I told him, after finishing my final slice.

'Hey, what's with the missing half-star?!' he asked.

'It's because the head chef purposely smeared tomato sauce over my face, and I don't tend to expect that in a high-class establishment.'

'Oh, really?' He laughed, sticking his finger into the pot of sauce. 'Well, maybe that's part of the experience.'

He lunged at me, and I ducked out of his way, and then we chased each other around the kitchen . . .

By the end of the afternoon, we were both covered in tomato and my stomach hurt from laughing. Now I'm home and I'm still absolutely buzzing. I can't wait to tell the girls all about it!

7.27 p.m.

I was on such a high, but now I'm feeling kind of down.

I was just looking on Instagram and the girls have all been out at Globalls playing indoor crazy golf. There are, like, a million photos of them messing about and having fun. The weirdest thing, though, is that there's no mention of it on our WhatsApp group, so I'm really confused. How come I don't know anything about it?! Have they purposely tried to leave me out?

I don't know what to do. Should I message them and say I've seen the pics, or should I just ignore them?!

8.11 p.m.

Decided to message Jess:

ME: Hey, have fun today?

JESS: Yeh, we went to Globalls and did the Zootopia one, which I'd not done before – it was really fun!

ME: When did you decide to do that?

JESS: This morning. Why?

ME: There wasn't anything about it on the WhatsApp.

JESS: Oh yeh, Amber set up a new chat.

ME: A new chat without me???

JESS: Only because she knew you were busy, Lottie. You told us all you had plans, remember?

ME: I know. I just think it's a bit weird setting up a group without me. It would have been nice to know what you were doing, even if I couldn't come 😕

JESS: I think Amber probably thought you'd get annoyed with all the messages.

ME: Maybe.

JESS: Anyway, did you have a good day? Did you meet the parents?!

ME: Yeh, it was fab. I'll fill you in on all the details on Monday! x

JESS: Can't wait xx

THOUGHT OF THE DAY:
I mean, I guess that makes sense, but I still can't shake this strange feeling – a feeling that I'd been left out. It's silly, I know, but I can't help it.

SUNDAY 29 JANUARY

I was having the best ever dream. Daniel had come round to my house, and we were watching a movie together – a really good romcom. Then he turned to me and said, 'I really like you, Lottie – you know that, don't you?'

And I smiled and said, 'Yes, and I really like you too, Daniel.'

Then he leant over to kiss me. At first it was really nice, but then suddenly he started shoving his tongue in my mouth, and it was **DISGUSTING** and I screamed . . .

But, yeh, I was actually being snogged by my dog.

Then Mum comes in with Bella and Toby to see what the noise is all about. She did NOT look happy.

'What are you shouting about, Lottie? You've just woken us all up.'

'It was Pot Noodle! He was kissing me – with tongues!' I cried.

'Why are you letting him kiss you on the mouth? It's hardly very hygienic.'

'I'm not letting him, Mother! I was trying to sleep.'

Toby is clearly finding the whole thing very amusing. 'Sis, did you know how Pot Noodle cleans his bottom . . . after he takes a BIG FAT DUMP?'

OH GAWD.

I started retching and rubbing at my face, trying to remove all traces of his slobber, then I jumped up and ran to the bathroom, where I washed my face three times (inside and out) and brushed my teeth five times.

Still feel a bit queasy though!

MONDAY 30 JANUARY

Today was a big pile of poo.

Firstly, it did not make me feel much better about TQOEG when, in registration, Amber was going on and on about how funny Globalls had been and telling me all the 'hilarious' stories, like when Molly hit the ball the complete opposite way and nearly took a flamingo's head off.

When she asked me why I wasn't laughing, I said, 'I guess you had to be there,' and she got all snooty with me.

NOBODY asked about what I did on Saturday (even Jess), and when I tried to tell them a funny story about the pizza-making, Amber went, 'Look, Lottie. We are constantly hearing about how amazing Daniel is, but today is meant to be about me, for once – so maybe you should focus your energy on finding me the perfect boyfriend.'

The 'auditions' were at lunchtime, so after our fourth

period we got to our form room as quickly as we could, to help set up. We dragged a few desks into a line to make a place for us (the panel) to sit behind and then we dragged the rest of the desks to the edges of the room.

'Now I think we need four people on the panel,' said Amber, looking at us thoughtfully. 'So I pick, Jess, Molly, Poppy and myself.'

What?!?

'Why can't we have five people on the panel?' I asked, feeling pretty left out.

'I want to make sure we look professional, and I think five would be too many. They only have four on *The X-Factor* and *Britain's Got Talent*.'

'Sorry, did I miss the part where we were making a TV show?!' I said, putting my hands on my hips.

Amber tutted at me impatiently. 'We're not, but you know what I mean.'

I turned to the others for help, but they just shrugged and looked away. I get that everyone is trying to be extra nice to Amber right now, but why does it feel like I always get the worst deal?

'Well, what am I meant to do then?' I asked.

'You can show the contestants in . . .'

'Contestants?! I thought you said this *wasn't* a TV show.'

'Lottie, you are the one who keeps going on about it being a TV show, not me!'

I sighed. It's impossible to win an argument against Amber. 'Fine, I'll show the *contestants* in. Anything else I should do, BOSS?'

'Not really. I suppose you can chat to them beforehand – a bit like a less funny, female version of Ant or Dec.'

The rest of TQOEG burst out laughing at that and I felt my face burn. It stung, being laughed at like that by my friends.

I turned round and walked out of the room, to check out how many boys had arrived. Not bad – there were seven.

I poked my head back round the door. 'Seven boys are here already!' I told them. I actually thought that was pretty impressive, but Amber just pulled a face and muttered something about expecting more.

I began showing them in, one by one, and most of the auditions lasted only seconds, because Amber was pretty harsh. From the other side of the door, I heard her barking her feedback at them.

'Weird voice!'

'Too annoying.'

'Too geeky!'

'Get a haircut!'

'Bad shoes!'

Considering it wasn't *The X-Factor*, Amber did a pretty good job of impersonating Simon Cowell!

The sixth 'contestant' was Burger Tom.

'Are you sure you want to do this, Tom?' I asked him before he went in.

He smiled. 'Yeh – what have I got to lose?'

'I dunno . . . your dignity, your confidence, your self-esteem?'

'As long as I've got enough time to get to the canteen afterwards, then I'm happy.'

There is no helping some people, so I sent him in.

Amber took one look at poor Burger Tom and yelled . . .

I expected him to be a little sad, but he just looked at his watch and said, 'At least I've still got fifteen minutes of lunch break left – I can probably bosh three burgers in that! Oh, by the way, I love your earmuffs – they look delicious.'

I laughed. 'Thanks, Tom.'

'LOTTIE!' Amber was shouting at me.

I poked my head round the door.

'This is getting ridiculous. How many are left?'

'Um, only one,' I told her.

She groaned, 'What a massive waste of my time.'

'And mine,' I muttered under my breath.

'Send him in then.'

I showed the last guy in. He was good-looking, tall, with short dark hair and tanned skin. He seemed very sure of himself – definitely the most promising of the bunch (if you like that sort of thing).

'I'm Casper,' he announced to the group, 'and I'm in Year Nine.'

Amber practically fell off her chair.

'Hi, Casper,' she said in her silly high-pitched voice.

Ladies and gentlemen – we had a winner!

Amber did not waste any time. She and Casper were Instagram official about seven minutes later. I had to admit it was a good photo of them both, but he didn't look quite so thrilled about it . . .

Me n' BAE ♥
♥ 237 likes
☺ You Guys!! ♥♥♥
☺ Too cute ☺

Amber kept refreshing the pic about every five seconds. 'Guys, guys . . . have you seen . . . our photo has got two hundred and thirty-seven likes!'

We all murmured our congrats.

'I think that makes us *officially* the cutest couple in school!' she said to the gang but while looking at me in particular.

I remembered how Molly had said the exact same thing about me and Daniel at the start of term, but I wasn't about to get into a debate with her over it – it wasn't a competition as far as I was concerned. So, I just smiled sweetly while Amber spent the rest of the day positively gloating about how amazing and gorgeous and perfect Casper is – oh, and did you know that he's **FOURTEEN** years old?!

I do, because she told me about seventy billion times.

After school, Jess came back to mine to work some more on our bee project. We had the structure and needed to divide the different sections between us, which we would each research and present. I was finding it quite difficult to concentrate though, because Amber's attitude today was still bugging me.

'Would you rather do "What's causing the bee population to decline?" or "What we can do to help bees"?' asked Jess, who was busy researching on my laptop.

When I didn't immediately reply, she said, 'Lottie, are you even listening to me?!'

'Yes, I said – it's just . . . I'm getting quite sick of Amber.'

Jess sighed, clearly frustrated I was getting distracted. 'How come?'

'She's so bossy and sometimes she can be pretty mean, especially to –'

Jess interrupted me: 'Lottie, remember she's going through a difficult time at home, so we need to be there for her.'

'She doesn't seem that bothered, Jess.'

'Just because she says she's not bothered, doesn't mean

she's not finding it hard.'

'But how is it OK to take it out on me?'

'Are you sure you're not imagining it? I know she can be pretty . . . direct, but I think she's grown up a lot recently – she's been so supportive about me coming out. I don't know what I would have done without her.'

I clenched my jaw. Jess didn't say it, but I'm sure she was thinking that it was Amber who went with her to the LGBTQ+ meeting last week – not me.

'Yeh,' I said. 'You're right. I'm probably just imagining it.'

Jess smiled. 'Good, now let's get to work – how about I research why there's a decline in bees and you do how we can help them?'

'Sure, sounds good to me,' I said. 'Let's get buzzin'!'

Jess laughed. 'Could you *BEE* any more cringe?'

'Chill, I'm only *pollen* your leg.'

'*Bee-hive* yourself, Lottie – we've got work to do!'

'Jess, you are such a *buzz-kill*.'

'You've better *bee-lieve* it, honey,' she said, winking at me, before we both collapsed in a fit of giggles.

TUESDAY 31 JANUARY

A bit of (not very nice) drama to report today.

Amber and Casper are over – or, as it turns out, they never really got started because it was just a big joke. I guess I'd better start from the beginning . . .

Amber came to school wearing a full face of make-up and so much perfume that it was difficult to breath if you stood close to her.

'I'm meeting my boyfriend for lunch today,' she told us, and then spent the whole of break time telling us about it! I didn't really mind, because her good mood meant she didn't make any more digs at me. Plus, I was trying to take Jess's advice and be more chill about the whole thing.

When the bell rang for lunch, she made us all come with her to meet Casper by the basketball courts. 'Maybe you can try to get a picture of us together,' she told us. 'If it's not too obvious, of course.'

She strode confidently ahead as we all followed behind, and as we approached the courts we could see him and his mates, a mix of Year Nine boys and girls, gathered in a big group. Amber stopped in her tracks, suddenly looking a little unsure. I guess she was expecting him to be on his own.

'What's wrong?' asked Molly.

'Nothing's wrong,' Amber replied.

'Do you want us to come with you?' asked Jess.

'No. I'm not a baby.'

Amber was trying to sound confident and sure of herself, but the slight wobble in her voice gave her away.

'It's OK to be nervous,' I said.

'I'm not nervous!!' she barked at me.

Then, without another word, she walked over while we watched, taking our phones out of our pockets ready to take a photo. A couple of Casper's mates nudged him as Amber approached. He looked up, but instead of getting up to greet her, he just sat there.

Amber stopped a couple of metres in front of the group, as if she was frozen to the spot. What on earth was going on?!

Next, it looked like Casper said something to her and then he and all his mates started laughing. A couple of them gave him pats on the back and fist bumps. TUMGG were standing near the group, and they must have heard everything, because they joined in with the laughing too.

For a while Amber just stood there, and then suddenly she turned round and started striding back towards us – her cheeks were red and she looked really shocked.

I'm not sure if I've ever seen Amber look so embarrassed?!.

'Amber, are you OK?' asked Poppy, running up and putting her arm round her.

'I'm fine!' she said, shrugging Poppy's arm off. 'I need the toilet. I'll see you later.' And then she walked off, leaving us totally confused.

'Shall we go after her?' asked Jess.

'I don't know,' said Molly. 'Maybe she needs a bit of time for herself.'

I looked back at Casper, who was still laughing and joking with his friends. 'What do you think happened?' I asked.

'I'm not sure,' replied Poppy, 'but I don't think it was anything good.'

So me and the girls headed to the canteen for lunch. We expected Amber to join us, but she never showed up. Afterwards we looked for her in the toilets and our form room, but she wasn't there either. She wasn't in her afternoon lessons and she was nowhere to be

found after school. It was as if she had totally
vanished.

4.13 p.m.

TQOEG WhatsApp group:

POPPY: Amber, where did you go? We didn't see
you after lunch . . .

4.21 p.m.

ME: Did something happen with Casper,
Amber? Hope you are OK!

4.33 p.m.

JESS: Please reply, Amber – we are getting
worried xxx

4.39 p.m.

MOLLY: Amber – where are you?! We are all here
for you if you need to talk xx

4.45 p.m.

ARGH! We are all getting seriously freaked out by Amber's lack of response. I mean, it's not like her to not look at her phone for an ENTIRE THIRTY-TWO MINUTES!!

Oh, hang on – my phone just pinged . . .

5.07 p.m.

AMBER: Chill out, guys!!! I'm fine. Got bad period pains so went home early – that's all.

POPPY: Oh phew!! I'm glad it was just period pain – I was starting to worry that you'd been kidnapped!

JESS: Or you'd fallen down a really deep well!

ME: Or got trapped in the janitor's closet and were getting eaten to death by rats!

AMBER: How would I get kidnapped from school?! What well did you think I'd fallen down?! I'd never even go in the janitor's closet because ewwwww, but if I did somehow end up in there, then I'd be punching those rats in the face before they could even take a tiny bite of me.

ME: You can't go around punching rats in the face, Amber! ☹ 👞

AMBER: Oh sorry, is that bad manners, Lottie? Should I provide them with a knife, fork and napkin before they turn me into an all-you-can-eat buffet?!

MOLLY: Well, I was a bit more logical about it 😂 – are you feeling better now, Amber?

AMBER: Yeh, had some Nurofen and been watching some Friends in bed.

POPPY: Sounds LUSH!

ME: But, hang on a minute – what happened with Casper?

AMBER: Dumped him.

MOLLY: What? Why?!

AMBER: Walked up to him and saw him in daylight for the first time. Not a pretty sight – like TOTALLY beneath me. So I thought . . . this is NEVER going to work. I could string him along or I could put him out of his misery there and then. So that's what I did.

JESS: OMG! Right to his face?!

AMBER: Yep.

POPPY: Was he upset?? And what did he say?

AMBER: Probably, yeh. He tried to laugh it off, trying to save face in front of his mates, I reckon.

MOLLY: That's a shame, Amber – you were so excited about it yesterday 😕

AMBER: Yeh well, that was yesterday. Anyway gotta go – I'm watching The One with the Prom Video and it's my fave.

POPPY: Oooh enjoy! I love that one! x

THOUGHT OF THE DAY:

I cannot work Amber out! But something feels a bit fishy about what she's just told us. Could she really have changed her mind so quickly? Why did she look so shocked and upset after she dumped him? Plus, it's a bit weird to just disappear like that without telling anyone, even if it was a really bad period. Maybe we'll find out more tomorrow.

WEDNESDAY I FEBRUARY

Well, today Amber acted as if nothing had happened.

Poppy tried to ask her for more details about . . . let's call it *The Incident*, in tutor time, but Amber shut her down immediately and changed the subject. It was clear that Amber didn't want to speak about it again, so we had to stop asking. The most annoying thing about it was that her mean side came back with a vengeance, and, again, it seemed to be targeted at me.

Here is a list of the things she did today:

* Pointed out a spot on my nose to everyone.
* Ignored everything I said and spoke over me.
* Laughed when I got hit in the face with a netball in PE.
* Pulled a face and rolled her eyes when someone complimented my earmuffs.
* Pushed in front of me in the canteen queue and then ordered the last cheese-and-bacon panini!!

* Spent ALL day glued to Jess's side being super sweet and lovely to her.

I know that last one sounds nice because everyone *should* be super sweet and lovely to Jess. But it was such a contrast to her behaviour towards me that I'm one hundred per cent sure that her main purpose was to make me feel left out.

Jess went to the LGBTQ+ club at lunchtime and, although I said that I'd like to go with her this time, she said she felt confident enough to go alone. I felt a little disappointed as I wanted to support her, like Amber did last week, but I guess it was good that she didn't feel she needed it.

We all went to meet her in the corridor afterwards though and I finally got to meet Cleo. They were quite tall, with short curly brown hair, and beautiful light-brown skin with a few freckles over the bridge of their nose. They had a wide, friendly smile, and I liked them right away.

Cleo

'Hi, Cleo,' said Amber, greeting her like an old friend.

'I think you've met everyone else,' said Jess, 'but this is my bestie, Lottie.'

I was thrilled that she'd introduced me as her bestie. 'Hi, Cleo,' I said, sticking my hand out and immediately regretting it – I mean, what kind of teenagers shake each other's hands?!

I knew Amber was smirking next to me, but Cleo took my hand and didn't make me feel awkward. 'Hi, Lottie, I've seen you around. I love the burger earmuffs, very kawaii.'

I grinned. 'Thanks!'

'Oh, guys,' said Jess excitedly. 'Cleo has tickets to the Bad Pancakes on Saturday too.'

'That's brilliant,' said Molly.

'Cool!' said Poppy.

Keen to be friendly, I turned to Jess and said, 'Maybe she could come with us?'

'Lottie!' Amber gasped loudly. 'Cleo goes by the pronouns "they" and "them", remember!'

'So . . . sorry,' I stuttered.

My face burned.

'It's fine, Lottie,' said Cleo. 'It can be hard to get it right at first.'

'I didn't mean –'

Cleo waved their hand dismissively and gave me another wide smile. 'No offence taken, honestly.'

I was really grateful that Cleo was so chill about it, but I still felt a bit embarrassed that I had got it wrong – and annoyed at Amber (again) for making it into a big deal.

4.57 p.m.

Poppy created group 'Rumours'

Poppy added you

POPPY: Have you heard??

JESS: Heard what???

POPPY: About what happened yesterday with Amber . . . Apparently TUMGG overheard everything, and they are spreading a rumour around school.

ME: What's the rumour?

POPPY: That Amber didn't dump Casper. That Casper came along to the auditions as a dare!

MOLLY: OMG, that's awful!!

ME: Who does that?! 😣

POPPY: AND then he asked her to meet him for lunch just to laugh at her. Apparently when she turned up, he said, 'I only did it for a laugh. You wouldn't seriously expect ME to go out with YOU, would you?!' in front of EVERYONE!

JESS: 😱 NOOOO!

MOLLY: I feel terrible for her 😞

ME: But why didn't she tell us?!

POPPY: Because she was humiliated, I guess.

JESS: And do you think that's why she went AWOL yesterday? Maybe she didn't have period pains after all . . .

POPPY: Yeh, I reckon so.

ME: What do you think we should do, girls?

JESS: We need to come up with a plan! X

So now I get why Amber's been so off with me today!!

I can't even imagine how embarrassing that must have been . . . Well, actually I can because it is the sort of thing that happens to me with frightening regularity, BUT it never happens to people like Amber! That's just not the way the way the universe is meant to work.

Although I can't pretend I'm Amber's biggest fan at the moment, I feel for her big time and I'm going to try my best to be a good friend and help her through it.

SO our plan is that tomorrow we are all going ice-skating to help put a smile back on her face. Everyone chipped in a little pocket money to buy her ticket for her! The extra good thing about this plan is that I'd also promised to go skating with Jess, so I can kill two birds with one stone!

THOUGHT OF THE DAY:
I actually hate that phrase and I apologize profusely (ooh, good word) for using it.

THURSDAY 2 FEBRUARY

Well, today didn't start too well because unfortunately we came face to face with TUMGG at break time.

'Shame about you and Casper,' Candice said, laughing.

'Yeh, you must be mortified,' smirked Izzy G.

Amber stared straight ahead and didn't even look at them.

'I'm starving,' she announced loudly to me, Poppy, Molly and Jess. 'Shall we go get a tray bake?'

I mean, she *must* have heard them, but she acted like they weren't even there, so we all nodded and ignored them too.

We got millionaire's shortbread at the canteen, and as we wolfed them down (they are so delicious) we revealed to Amber that we'd organized a surprise ice-skating trip. Although she was curious as to why we'd booked it for her, we just said it was to thank her for all the lovely takeaways she's bought us recently, which she seemed to accept – phew!

We are never going to admit that we know what happened with Casper, because I think she'd hate that. Fingers crossed the gossip will die down soon anyway.

I'm really looking forward to tonight and hoping it's a chance for me and Amber to . . . I don't know really . . . kind of make up, I guess? Even though we haven't officially fallen out, there's a strange atmosphere between us and I want to squash it once and for all.

Right, off to have an early dinner before skating – BYE! x

5.37 p.m.

PLOT TWIST – I'm in the car on my way to A&E!!

What happened was . . . I was eating my tea (sausage, chips and sweetcorn – yum) and for some unknown reason I picked up a piece of sweetcorn and put it up my nose. It went further than I meant it to (not that I meant it to go up there at all – I mean, who *means* to get sweetcorn stuck up their noses?!) But anyway . . .

309

suddenly I started to panic a bit and I tried to snort it out, but I accidentally sniffed it even further up my nostril and then it was properly stuck.

I was sort of frozen at that point, and Mum started looking at me funny and said, 'Is everything OK, Lottie?'

And I said, 'Yes, yes. I'm fantastic,' but then my eyes started streaming, and it felt so uncomfortable so I just had to say . . . 'I put a bit of sweetcorn up my nose, and it won't come out.'

Toby obvs thought this was totes hilar, but Mum was not particularly amused.

Anyway, long story short . . . The Fun Police tried to flush it out and breathe it out, and then they tried to dislodge it with a pair of tweezers, but nothing worked. In fact, everything we tried only seemed to push it in deeper and deeper.

Dad called 111 and then, after he'd answered about a million questions about whether I was dying or not, they said that the best thing to do would be to go to A&E, which Dad was not very happy about because he had just poured himself a nice glass of Malbec.

I said, 'What's more important? Wine or your daughter being in considerable pain?'

He said he didn't want to answer that and that he'd have a lot more sympathy if I hadn't been directly responsible for putting a piece of sweetcorn up my nose in the first place.

I'm so sad for myself because I was really looking forward to ice-skating, and I keep trying to think of someone else to blame but there is no one. Only me, and I hate having to blame myself – it doesn't seem fair.

6.12 p.m.

TQOEG WhatsApp group:

ME: I'm sorry I'm going to miss tonight, girls – I'm in A&E!

JESS: OMG!! What happened?! Are you OK?

ME: No, I'm in pain. Something bad has happened to my nose.

MOLLY: Oh no – what did you do to your nose?!

ME: No one knows yet. I'm waiting to be seen by the doctor.

AMBER: Sounds weird – what are your symptoms?

ME: It hurts and I can't breathe properly.

JESS: I'm so sorry to hear that, Lottie. That sounds really serious! 😱

POPPY: OMG, don't you need to breathe to be alive?????

AMBER: Yes, Poppy, breathing is kind of essential.

POPPY: OH NO, LOTTIE! ARE YOU GONNA DIE??

ME: NO! Don't worry, I'm not going to die. It's nothing serious, I don't think. Just perhaps some sort of an obstruction.

MOLLY: Phew, do they know what the obstruction might be?

ME: No, not . . . yet.

AMBER: Maybe a spider crawled up it? You do have rather large nostrils.

ME: Thanks, Amber.

JESS: Sending lots of love and hugs, Lottie. Let us know as soon as you are seen! xxxxxxxxxx

ME: Thanks – will do xx

I'm feeling a bit bad now for being . . . shall we say, slightly fuzzy with the truth. I mean, I've worried my friends (well, Poppy at least) that something serious might be wrong when it's all self-inflicted – eeeek.

8.21 p.m.

I've been triaged now, which is where the doctors assess your injury and decide when you will be treated, depending on how serious it is. Turns out that having put a bit of sweetcorn up your own nostril is not particularly serious, so I will be waiting a long time!!

9.44 p.m.

Three kids have come in with broken bones and they got bumped above me, even though I've been here for, like, three hours! Very unfair.

11.56 p.m.

In the car on the way home. Dad is giving me the silent treatment.

The whole experience was . . . hideous?! Firstly, the

doctor who was treating me (and my nostril) was young and kind of cute. He introduced himself as Dr Granger. Then he asked me what the problem was . . .

I don't think I have ever blushed harder in my entire life and that is saying something, because we all know how regularly I blush!

Dr Granger tried a few techniques to get the sweetcorn out – firstly, with some long spiky tweezer things, but he couldn't get a good enough grip. Next, he tried this suction thingy, which didn't work either, but all that poking around up in my nose had made it feel really itchy . . . so then I did a massive sneeze and the corn just flew out.

That's good news, I hear you say. Well . . . it would have been except that the corn had created a sort of bogey floodgate, which burst and propelled the corn out at super speed along with about five hundred litres of my own snot that hit Dr Granger's nice white clean uniform!!!

OH MY LIFE, I WAS MORTIFIED.

He was very gracious about it though. Said he rarely goes home without being covered in some sort of bodily fluid – gross.

The worst bit? The absolute worst part is that he then gave me a lecture about putting things up my nose and how dangerous it was. Apparently I could have caused damage to my septum or a serious infection. He also said that he'd seen a lot of toddlers who have been into A&E for putting things up their noses, but he's never had to treat a teenager before.

MEGA CRINGE.

Dr Granger then put the sweetcorn in a little plastic tube and said, 'Would you like to keep this?'

I think he was actually joking, but also I kind of wanted it so I said, 'Yes, please,' in a very quiet voice.

I thought back to my New Year's resolutions . . .

9. Try not to be quite so weird.

MAJOR FAIL.

Why am I so weird?! WHY?!?!

On the way home, I said to Dad, 'You know what
Dr Granger said about getting covered in bodily fluids?
Well, that has put me right off being a doctor.'

'Probably for the best, Lotts,' he replied. 'Putting
sweetcorn up your nose for fun suggests you may
not have the required brain cells anyway.'

Then he laughed all the way home – how very rude is
that?!

Maybe I will become a doctor after all, just to prove
him wrong.

FRIDAY 3 FEBRUARY

Had a terrible dream that I couldn't stop putting things up my nose. Every time I went back to hospital, I had to see Dr Granger and he kept getting crosser and crosser with me for wasting NHS resources. I joined a group called Support For People Who Can't Stop Putting Things Up Their Nostrils (SFPWCSPTUTN) but that didn't help either – I was out of control. After a while, my nostrils got larger and larger because of all the stuff I'd put up them, and by the time I was fifteen they were so large that if you looked up them you could even see my brain. Dr Granger said that I was at breaking point, and if my nostrils got any larger, then my brain would fall out and I might die.

I tried very hard, I really did, but one day I absentmindedly put a tube of lip balm up there and that was the final straw – when Dr Granger removed it, my brain slid out too. By some miracle I didn't die, but my brain couldn't go back in, so it was put in a jar and I had to push it around in a trolley – I felt so exposed!

7.46 a.m.

I asked Mum at breakfast if there was a reason why I'd been having such crazy dreams lately and she suggested that it was probably too much screentime. Then she said that maybe she and Dad should review the parental controls on my phone (!!) – so I told her that her hair looked nice, grabbed my bag and ran out of the door.

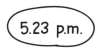

5.23 p.m.

The girls rushed up to me when I got to our form room this morning. Apparently they had been really worried something was seriously wrong.

When I reluctantly told them the reason why I had been in hospital was because I put a sweetcorn up my nose, and that the reason why I did it was – I HAVE NO IDEA?!?! Let's just say, their sympathy levels took a sharp decline.

They did find it quite funny though. Well, that was until Amber went, 'This all sounds pretty ridiculous, Lottie . . . Are you sure you weren't just making up an elaborate excuse because you wanted to see Daniel last night instead?'

Like, errr, HELLO, Amber? My entire life is a serious of ridiculous events – surely she should know that by now!!

The most annoying thing was that then the rest of the gang started looking at me suspiciously, like maybe Amber was right.

I put my hands on my hips. 'If I had to make up an excuse, why would I say that I ended up in hospital because I put a bit of sweetcorn up my *own* nose?! I would have said something much less embarrassing like I had a . . . I dunno, I had a headache or something.'

Amber narrowed her eyes. 'Well, maybe because it's some sort of double bluff!'

'I'm not that smart,' I argued. 'I don't even really know what a double bluff is.'

'She's right, Amber,' said Molly. 'She didn't even learn to tie her own shoelaces until she was nine.'

'Exactly! Thank you, Molly,' I said.

I could tell that I had most of the girls on side, but Amber was not backing down. 'Well, I'm not convinced. It all feels rather . . . convenient to me.'

I really didn't want to have to admit this, but I had no choice:

I've got the piece of sweetcorn in a plastic tube at home, if you want to see it!

It was an unfortunate time for the classroom to go completely silent.

'Look, I know it was stupid,' I told them, 'but it was a genuine mistake. I really wanted to be there with you all last night. I'm really sad I missed it.'

'It doesn't matter, Lottie,' said Jess. 'We've got tomorrow night to look forward to, haven't we?'

I nodded eagerly. I was excited too . . . except for one

tiiiiiiny little thing. I still hadn't told the girls about me going with Daniel, and I had a funny feeling that it wasn't going to go down too well.

After school, we went to Frydays as per tradition. Amber was still acting funny with me, mostly by ignoring me and shutting down my attempts at conversation, so when Daniel came in with Theo and they made their way over to us, I was really glad.

I told them about what happened last night and, even though they laughed, they believed me.

'Is your nose OK now?' Daniel asked.

I rubbed it. 'It's still a bit sore,' I told him, realizing that none of TQOEG had even asked that, because Amber had derailed the whole convo into making me look bad.

'Well, I know what will make it better,' he said, grabbing my hand and walking me over to the counter. 'Can I have a battered sausage and chips, please?' Daniel asked the server.

I looked at him and grinned. Not that I was going to tell

him but battered sausage and chips is the very top of the Chipometer of Love – we were destined to be soulmates!! EEK.

When the food arrived, I held it up excitedly to the girls, who were huddled in a group outside with Theo sharing a big bag of chips. I pointed at the sausage and mouthed, *Soulmates*, at them.

Jess and Molly raised their eyebrows and Poppy smiled, but then Amber whispered something to them. Theo nodded and they quickly turned away.

I tried to enjoy my sausage and chips after that, but it was hard. I wanted to ask Daniel if he'd noticed anything strange, but he seemed pretty oblivious to it all.

THOUGHT OF THE DAY:
I'm convinced that Amber is trying to create a divide within the group. I feel like she wants me out of TQOEG and I don't know what to do!!

SATURDAY 4 FEBRUARY

Woke up early feeling stressed. The concert is tonight, and I've still got a major problem in that I am meant to be going with both Daniel AND the girls but I've not told either of them about the other.

Before you say it, I know what you are thinking: *In your last diary, after the surprise Antoine Christmas day debacle* (OOH good vocab, Lottie) *you said, and I quote:*

'It's always best to be honest and not put off owning up to stuff – even bad stuff. The longer you leave it, the worse it will get – trust me!'

Have you learnt nothing, Lottie?!

No. I. Have. Not.

Don't judge me, OK? I never said I was perfect, did I? If you are hoping to read the adventures of a person who overcomes a series of unfortunate events, with a clear story arc and meaningful character development, then continue **AT YOUR PERIL**.

If you want to read about a person who makes the same mistakes again AND again, and learns absolutely nothing, then I'm your gal.☺

Perhaps I should wear some sort of warning sign around my neck? A bit like the ones you see in hotels or restaurant toilets . . .

Apologies for the ongoing renovation work. We hope it will be complete Soon ☺

So, the way I see it, I have a few choices:

1. Come clean to Daniel and go with the girls.

2. Come clean to the girls and go with Daniel.

3. Clone myself. Someone must have invented a cloning/duplication machine by now, right?! Didn't they do that with a sheep already?!

4. Find my doppelganger (everyone has at least one apparently)!

5. Go back in time to the point when I was a mere egg and divide myself in two, so that I now have an identical twin.

6. Snort another piece of sweetcorn and end up in A&E again.

I'm not very keen on options 1 or 2 (for obvious reasons). There are a few ethical issues and time constraints involved with options 3 to 6 but one of them has gotta come good, surely?!?

Was just googling 'cloning machines' when a message pops up on our TQOEG WhatsApp group:

POPPY: OMG, I'M SO EXCITED ABOUT OUR #GirlsNight!

JESS: EEK IT'S GONNA BE THE BEST NIGHT EVER #GirlPower

AMBER: BOYS ARE RUBBISH #GirlsRuleTheWorld

MOLLY: CAN'T WAIT TO BUST SOME MOVES WITH YOU #GirlsWinBoysInTheBin

ME: Bit sexist maybe? But yay – looking forward to it! See ya later! x

MOLLY: Er, Lottie, are you not excited????????

ME: Yeh, obvs I'm excited!

AMBER: You don't sound very excited . . .

POPPY: Why aren't you using caps??

JESS: And why don't you have a hashtag?!??!?!

ME: Oh um. Soz. OK . . . I'M REALLY REALLY REALLY REALLY REALLY REALLY REALLY REALLY REALLY REALLY EXCITED #GIRLSNIGHTSARETHEBESTNIGHTSEVER!!!!!

AMBER: Better.

DAMMIT. DAMMIT. DAMMIT!!!!

(10.23 a.m.)

ARGH. Time machines don't actually exist – *Back to the Future* was just a pack of lies!!!

(10.44 a.m.)

DANIEL: Hey, you looking forward to later? The Bad Pancakes are SO good live – you are going to love them!

ME: Hey, yeh, I'm looking forward to it as much as a trip to the dentist to get my braces tightened!

DANIEL: Isn't that a bad thing?! 😕

ME: Not if you are excited about getting really straight teeth!

DANIEL: Right . . . weird.

11.21 a.m.

Got Dad to tweet a photo of me on Twitter. Told him I was investigating doppelgangers for a science project:

> My daughter wants to see if she can find her doppelganger. Anyone out there look like her? Please share a photo! Please retweet!

1.45 p.m.

It got 327 retweets and 1.5k likes!! About fifteen people shared pictures. Some didn't look AT ALL like me: one was a photo of a middle-aged man with a beard, and another person shared a photo of a piece of cutlery?! Rude!

Wow — she looks exactly like my favourite teaspoon — I drew a face on it with felt-tip pen to help you visualize the resemblance:

One was pretty convincing though, especially if I could persuade the girl in it to wear a red hairband. However, she also turned out to be a twelve-year-old from Iceland and I wasn't sure the flight timings would work. I guess her parents might also think it was a bit odd.

2.12 p.m.

Getting desperate now. Went to the freezer to get some frozen sweetcorn but couldn't find any. No tins in the cupboard either.

'Muuuuuuuuuum . . . do we have any sweetcorn anywhere?'

'No, we are all out.'

'Peas?'

'What do you want peas for?! You don't even like them!'

'No reason.'

'I hope you are not planning anything silly, Lottie?'

'Of course not!!'

Went to Toby's room and tried putting a 1x1 Lego up my nostril, but it was too ouchy, so I had to give up. Why, oh why is my life so difficult?

Decided to ask my psychic fishy-wishy for advice . . .

Felicity is right – I have to put my biggest girl pants on.
I'm going to call Daniel and tell him that I'm sorry but
I'm going to the concert with my girls! They need me
more than he does, and I know it's the right thing to do.

3.09 p.m.

Just going to have a KitKat Chunky first and work up the confidence . . .

3.15 p.m.

Or maybe two KitKat Chunkys and a cheeky Pot Noodle – oops.

3.44 p.m.

I called him and it was fine!

I was honest and said that I'd accidentally got myself in this tricky situation, because I didn't want to let anyone down, but I thought, after careful consideration, that it was more important for me to go with my friends – and do you know what he said?!

He said, 'Don't worry – that's cool, Lottie. TBH Theo's been a bit annoyed that I didn't invite him to the gig, so I'll ask him instead.'

I can't believe it was so simple – phew!

AMBER: DISASTER! My dad forgot about the concert and he's made plans to go out with a friend 🙁

JESS: What?! Can't he cancel??

AMBER: No, apparently I'm not that important.

MOLLY: That sucks, Amber.

POPPY: 🙁 🙁 🙁

ME: What are we gonna do? Can anyone else's parents take us?

POPPY: My mum and dad are going out for dinner.

JESS: My mum can't leave my little sister.

MOLLY: We won't all fit in our tiny car.

ME: We've got a seven-seater. I'll ask . . .
Hang on.

JESS: 🤞 🤞 🤞

MOLLY: Come on, Mummy and Daddy
Brooks 🙏

I went downstairs to find Mum and Dad. On the one hand I
was really hoping one of them would be able to take us to
the concert, but on the other hand I was dreading them
having to be there. Especially Dad – I just knew he'd do
something super cringy and embarrass me, and that would
mean one more thing to worry about.

Everyone was in the kitchen. Mum was clattering about
making tea, Dad was playing a game of Downfall with Toby,
and Bella was sitting in Pot Noodle's bed with him, 'reading'
him a story.

'I don't suppose . . . one of you could take me and the girls to
the concert tonight, could you? Amber's dad can't any more,'
I said.

Dad sighed. 'I gave up my night for you yesterday – taking you to hospital, remember.'

'Yeh, I know – sorry.'

'What time would I need to drop you off and pick you up?'

'Well . . . that's the thing. Under-18s need a parent chaperone, so you'd have to come to the concert too . . .'

Dad visibly perked up. 'Oooh, now you're talking – it's been a long time since I've been to a gig!'

'Well, obviously you could just stay in the foyer and –'

'Stay in the foyer like some kind of saddo?! I'll be busting my best moves, my girl.'

I was pretty horrified, but I didn't have time to argue. I dashed back to my room to let the girls know.

ME: Panic over. My dad can take us.

POPPY: Wahooooo! Amazing!! Love your dad!

MOLLY: Bill Brooks is a lifesaver!!

JESS: Big thanks to your dad – he's the best!

ME: 😃 😃 😃 Come round mine @ 5.30 for dinner and drinks! X

POPPY: YAY! See you soooooooooon x

Amber gave my messages a thumbs up but didn't say a thing. At first I thought that was a bit rude, but then I realized that maybe she felt embarrassed that my dad was taking us, because her dad forgot . . .

11.22 p.m.

Sorry, I know it's late, but I also know that you've probably been waiting around, dying for an update and, you know me, I don't like to disappoint.

Firstly – the Bad Pancakes were **EPIC!!** OMG, I'm now a MEGA fan!! I think my legs are going to absolutely kill tomorrow from all the dancing I did.

But let me start at the beginning . . .

All the girls came round to my house for pizza and
mocktails. We asked Alexa to play some Bad Pancakes
songs and we danced around my room, swigging virgin
piña coladas. It was muchos funos!

When it was time to go, we all piled into Dad's car and
he drove us to the Music Hall. The queue was already
massive by the time we arrived and it was SO cold too.
I was really annoyed with myself for not listening to
Mum about taking my BIG coat (but shhhhh don't tell
her that).

We were all really glad when we finally got in. First stop was the merch stand, where we all got super-cool matching tees . . . You like?

Dad bought us all Cokes and then promised to stand at the back and keep his distance for the rest of the night. There was a support act on first called Fridge Of Doom (seriously, where do they get their names from?). They were pretty good and we all got quite into them, but when the Bad Pancakes came on, the whole crowd went absolutely wild! I've never been to a proper gig before and the atmosphere was amazing.

They have this really cool song called 'Stuck to the Ceiling'. It must have been one of their most popular songs, because everyone seemed to know the words and was singing along. We all threw our hands in the air – Amber looked like she was having a great time and for a moment I completely forgot there was any atmosphere between us at all.

I spotted Cleo dancing with a friend just a few metres away from us. I pointed them out to Jess, but she was too shy to ask them to come over, so Amber stepped in and practically dragged them over to our group. Their friend was called Lola, and they both seemed pretty pleased to see us.

The next song was called 'Lemon 'n' Sugar', which was super upbeat, followed by a very catchy 'Don't Spill the Batter, Baby'. The only problem was that these songs were making me SO hungry. I mean, who doesn't like a pancake?! Yummy.

I looked behind me to check that my dad was behaving and he was nowhere to be seen. Confused, I scanned the crowd to try to find him. I was scared he would be doing something embarrassing and I was not wrong.

He was right at the blummin' front like a groupie.
And that's not all – he must have also snuck off to the
merch stand, because he was now the proud owner of a
Bad Pancakes T-shirt and he was playing air guitar in it!

I swallowed hard, hoping and praying that no one else
had seen him, but unfortunately it was not to be.

I felt a hand grab mine. 'Your dad is brilliant,' Daniel
shouted above the music.

'That's not exactly how I'd describe him,' I said. 'I told
him to stay at the back and not to embarrass me!'

'Lottie, that's mean! See how much fun he's having!' Daniel laughed.

I smiled. Dad did look like he was having an absolute blast, which I guess was kind of endearing (or well, it would be, if it was someone else's dad!).

'So,' continued Daniel, 'I know you're with the girls, but have you got time to dance with me for a bit?'

'Um, I . . .'

'Lottie! Daniel!' Amber appeared between us, putting her arms round both our necks. 'You guys are sooooooo cute together – are you having a good night?'

I frowned. Why was she suddenly being super friendly?!

'Yeh. They're sick, aren't they?' said Daniel, nodding his head towards the band.

'Always,' said Amber, smiling at us both.

I turned to Daniel. 'I'd better go back with Amber and find the girls.'

'Can't you stay for a bit?' he asked.

'Lottie, chill. We're fine,' said Amber. 'In fact, that's what I came to tell you. Jess has gone off with Cleo, and me and the others are going to find somewhere to sit down because Poppy's feet are aching. You should stay here with Daniel and have fun – no one will mind.'

'I don't know. I think I shou–'

Daniel looked at me. 'Come on – just for a bit?'

I had been with the girls for the whole night so far, and if Jess and Cleo had gone off together, then surely it would be fine to spend a bit of time with Daniel?

'OK, just for a bit,' I said, smiling.

'Cool,' said Amber. 'We'll meet you back in our spot in twenty minutes.' Then she left, pushing her way back through the crowd.

The band started another track – 'American Blueberry', which I thought was my absolute fave, until they played 'Just Keep Flippin''. I don't think there was a single bad song all night. I was having so much fun that the time just seemed to disappear and Dexter, the lead singer, announced they were going to play the final song of the night, 'Stack 'Em Up'.

'Argh – I've got to find the girls,' I told Daniel. 'Can you help me?'

'Sure.'

We made our way through the crowd, back to the place where I'd been standing with the girls originally, but I couldn't see them anywhere. I looked at my watch – it was almost exactly twenty minutes since I'd last seen Amber, so she should have been waiting for me there.

'I'm sure it was here,' I said.

'Well, let's just wait here and enjoy the last song. Maybe they've gone to the toilet or something,' replied Daniel.

So we danced to the last song (FYI it was epic). When everyone started walking to the exits, the girls still weren't back. Me and Daniel looked around, but we couldn't see them anywhere, so we walked through to the foyer to check there. Straight away we saw them huddled by the main doors. Amber had her arm round Jess, and she didn't look happy.

'I'll see you later,' I told Daniel. I didn't think it would be good if we went over together.

'Bye, Lottie. I had a great time tonight,' he called after me.

'Me too.'

I walked up to my friends quickly. 'There you are,' I said. 'I've been looking for you all.'

'Bit late now, Lottie,' said Amber. 'The gig's over!'

I was stunned. 'What? You knew –'

'It was meant to be a girls' night out,' said Amber in a sad voice. 'But you went off with your boyfriend – *again!*'

'You told me to! You said that –'

'Don't blame me,' said Amber, holding her hands up. 'I said I was going back to our spot, and you said you wanted to stay with Daniel . . .'

'That's not what happened,' I said. I was getting so frustrated – why was she twisting things?

I looked at Jess, but she wouldn't even meet my eyes. That's when I noticed she was crying.

'Jess, what's wrong?' I asked, moving towards her and reaching my arms out.

Amber stepped between us, blocking me. 'Well, while you were with your *boyfriend*, Jess has had a bad night because it turns out that Lola is Cleo's girlfriend. But you wouldn't know that, would you? Because you ditched us.'

Now I was fuming. 'I didn't ditch you! It was your idea!'

Amber sighed. 'It's never your fault, is it?'

I looked at the other girls. 'Molly? Poppy?'

But they just shrugged, clearly confused about whose side they were supposed to take.

That's when Dad appeared. 'WOW!' he said. 'That was TOTALLY RAD, or actually . . . that was **TOTALLY SICK** – that's what you kids say these days, isn't it? Look, I even got my band T-shirt signed by Dexter!'

Even though that was kind of impressive, we all looked at him glumly.

'Blimey,' he continued, 'you guys look utterly pooped. Come on, let's head to the car park and get you all home.'

On the journey back, we all sat in silence. Well, I say silence, but Dad had put the Bad Pancakes on Spotify and was singing along at full volume. In typical embarrassing Dad style, he was getting all the words wrong – normally I would have been mortified, but tonight I was kind of glad, as it covered up the awkward silence between TQOEG and meant that we didn't have to speak to each other.

One by one, we dropped the girls off. They all thanked Dad for the lift but barely even glanced at me. When Amber got out, she said, 'Mr Brooks, I absolutely *loved* your rendition of "Stuck to the Pan". You have a *great* voice.' Then she gave me the most self-satisfied smirk I'd ever seen!

'Thanks, Amber,' said Dad. 'That's really kind of you to say, and call me Bill, please.'

'OK. Bye, Biiiiill,' she said in a cutesy voice.

After she'd shut the door, Dad turned to me and said, 'What a lovely girl! So sweet and polite.'

'Yeh, she really is,' I said.

When we finally arrived back at our house, after a quick chat with Mum I came right up to my room and got ready for bed. I'd had one of the best *and* one of the worst nights of my life, all rolled into one – and even after writing it all down for you, I'm still trying to figure out what really happened. I think the best thing to do is try to get some sleep and work things out in the morning.

(11.42 p.m.)

ARGH! I'm actually way too anxious to sleep. I know it's late, but I decided to message Jess:

> **ME:** You OK? I'm upset you are upset and I'm sorry I wasn't there.

> **JESS:** Not really. I feel really let down, Lottie.

> **ME:** I don't even know what I did! You can't blame me for the fact that Cleo has a girlfriend.

> **JESS:** I'm not – but we were meant to be on a girls' night and you went off with Daniel.

ME: I spent half the night with you and then I spent some time with him too – what's wrong with that?

JESS: What's wrong is that I never see you any more and, even when I do, you are only thinking about your boyfriend.

ME: Amber told me that you all said it was fine . . .

JESS: Why do you keep blaming Amber? It was your choice, and you chose him.

ME: I didn't – it's like Amber is purposely planning things for the gang to do on days when I've already made plans with Daniel. She's always trying to leave me out.

JESS: You are just being paranoid – and what about Thursday? You were meant to be there supporting her, but it seems that you only want to skate with your boyfriend.

ME: You can't blame me for not coming on Thursday! That was a medical emergency.

JESS: You can't call putting sweetcorn up your own nose on purpose a medical emergency.

ME: It wasn't on purpose – it was by mistake. There is a difference and you make it sound like I'm lying.

JESS: Well, maybe you were. Amber still thinks you made it all up.

I turned my bedroom light on, searching for the tube that I'd brought home from hospital. I found it and snapped a photo to send to Jess.

ME: Look – here is the ACTUAL piece of sweetcorn!

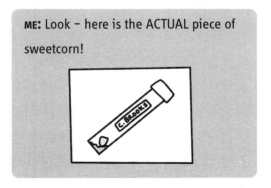

JESS: What's that green stuff at the bottom?

ME: My snot.

JESS: EWWWWW!

ME: Sorry, but I wanted to prove it to you.

JESS: That's not proof – you could have got that piece of sweetcorn out of the freezer right now and sneezed on it.

ME: You seriously think I'm lying?!

JESS: I don't know . . .

JESS: No, of course not.

JESS: I just don't know what to think any more. Amber says you've changed and she's right.

ME: Amber hates me. She's just trying to cause trouble!

JESS: She doesn't hate you. She's going through a hard time right now, Lottie, and you aren't being a very good friend to her.

ME: She's the one not being a very good friend to me!

JESS: Well, she's been a good friend to me . . .

She didn't need to say anything else. I know what she meant.

Jess thinks I've been a terrible friend – and maybe she's right?!

SUNDAY 5 FEBRUARY

A terrible night. I think it was about 3.a.m. before I finally got to sleep.

I just couldn't stop the horrible conversation I had with Jess swirling around in my brain. I kept going through different emotions: sometimes I felt upset and sad, and other times I felt cross and angry.

When I did finally drop off, I had a nightmare. It was like I was in that movie *Honey, I Shrunk the Kids* and I'd been turned into a teeny person. Mum was making pancakes and I fell into the batter when I was trying to get her attention. Then she tipped me into the pan and was frying me. She lifted the pan and flipped me high into the air . . .

That's when I woke up and realized I was actually a full-sized human in my bed and luckily not about to get fried to death . . . phew.

It didn't change anything though. I'm still in a poo situation that I don't know how to get out of.

The thing is, it's not that I don't want to admit that I'm wrong – I *know* I've made some mistakes, but I never meant to hurt anybody. It feels like Amber's jumping on every opportunity she can to try to make me look bad and it's just not fair.

(11.09 a.m.)

I remembered what Mum said about screentime causing strange dreams and I voluntarily (?!) asked Dad to put limits on my phone. That pancake dream was the final straw. I may regret it later.

(11.45 a.m.)

Already regretting it.

(2.22 p.m.)

OH GAWD!

I've just remembered that our bee assignment is due tomorrow. Obvs things with Jess are kind of weird but it's not like her to not mention it?!

(2.32 p.m.)

Decided to message her:

> **ME:** Hey, our bee assignment is due tomorrow, remember?

> **JESS:** Yeh. I know.

> **ME:** Do you want to get together this afternoon to go over it?

> **JESS:** We've split it out into sections, so I don't think we need to.

> **ME:** Don't you think it would be better if we rehearsed it though?

> **JESS:** I don't have time today. Just do your bit and I'll do mine. It'll be fine.

> **ME:** Don't you mean it'll *bee* fine?

She didn't even reply!!

359

6.49 p.m.

I spent the afternoon doing some final research and making cue cards for tomorrow. I know Jess will be well prepared and I don't want to let her down. I can't help feeling, though, that because we've not practised it, Miss Dodson is going to be suspicious that we've not worked on it together, which was a key part of the assignment.

I reckon it'll probably take two or three English lessons to get through all the presentations, so hopefully we won't have to do it tomorrow anyway – and that will give me more time to work things out with Jess (fingers crossed).

8.43 p.m.

Thought maybe I'd speak to Felicity for a bit of reassurance, but kinda wish I hadn't.

MONDAY 6 FEBRUARY

Unfortunately, Felicity was right on the money – it was a full-capitals kind of UTTER DISASTER.

Instead of working things out with Jess, I've made things even worse.

In English, Miss Dodson asked if anyone would like to go first with their presentation, but no one volunteered. I was trying to avoid eye contact, but maybe everyone else was too because she went, 'Hmm, let's see – I know, how about Lottie and Jess? I know I can always rely on you two.'

We walked slowly up to the front of the class, looking about as enthusiastic as oranges about to go through a pulper.

Jess cleared her throat and said, 'We have chosen the topic of bees and how they are becoming an endangered species. First of all, Lottie is going to talk about the decline of the bee population and then I'll talk about the ways in which we can help them.'

WHAT?! That is not what we agreed! We agreed that Jess would do the first section and I would do the second!

Didn't we?!? I was sure that's what we said.

I looked at Jess, panic in my eyes, but she frowned at me, clearly as confused as I was.

OH GAWD – I'd researched the wrong section, hadn't I! Ditsy Lottie wasn't paying attention and now she's messed everything up (again).

I looked around the classroom – all eyes were on me. They were waiting for me to say something.

I wasn't good at public speaking at the best of times, let alone when I had no clue what I was meant to be speaking about.

Miss Dodson coughed lightly and smiled at me, encouraging me to start.

'So, um, ah,' I stuttered, 'first a joke – who is a bee's favourite singer?'

Silence.

'It's Bee-yoncé! *Ba-doom-tish!*' I mimed hitting a drum and cymbal (but wish I hadn't).

More silence and a few groans.

'Right – bees, uh, well, we all like bees . . . I do
anyway . . . except when they sting . . . which is a bit
ouchy but . . . . yeh, uh . . . they're important cos they,
er . . . they, er, make honey – and they look cute!'

Words seemed to just be falling out of my mouth, and I
had very little control over what I was saying . . .

'Oh, and they can fly! And that's pretty cool, huh? I
mean, who wouldn't like to fly?!'

For some reason I then decided to lift my arms and start
flapping them around, as I did an impression of a bee.

Everyone burst out laughing (not in a good way) and
Miss Dodson had to tell them to be quiet. I could see
Jess out of the corner of my eye – she did not look
pleased.

I continued, 'But sadly . . . very sadly . . . bees are dying,
because of . . . well . . .'

Thirty pairs of eyes were staring at me, waiting for me
to go on, but I couldn't because I had no idea what I
was talking about.

There was nothing else I could do but hold my hands
up and come clean. 'I'm really sorry, miss, but I don't
actually know. I've researched the wrong bit – I thought
Jess was doing this part, so –'

'Well, this is very disappointing, girls,' Miss Dodson
said through tight lips.

'It's my fault,' I said. 'Jess was –'

'You are meant to be working on it together,' Miss
Dodson interrupted, 'so you should both be well
aware of which sections you were presenting.'

My cheeks started to burn, and tears pricked my eyes. It was horrible being told off like this in front of the whole class and I had to try really hard not to cry.

'Jess?' asked Miss Dodson, 'do you have anything to say?'

I snuck a look at Jess – she was staring at the floor. 'No, Miss,' she said so quietly, you could barely hear her.

Miss Dodson sighed and shook her head, 'Right, go and sit down. Alfie and Henry, let's have you two next, please.'

'Sorry,' I whispered to Jess as we sat back down, but she didn't reply. She just stared at the desk for the rest of the lesson. Another five or six pairs did their presentations after ours, but I can't tell you what any of them were about. I was too busy thinking about how I'd let Jess down (again) and how we'd get a terrible grade, and it was all my fault.

At the end of the lesson, Miss Dodson gave out score papers to each group. When she handed us ours, Jess didn't even reach for it. We got a U (AKA ungraded) and Miss Dodson had written: *An interesting subject choice that was poorly researched and prepared. It did not seem as if you had worked together on this project at all, so I had no choice but to fail you – disappointing!*

I saw Jess look at the score and then she just walked off, without saying anything.

When I got home, I was feeling pretty down. I slumped on to the sofa and Pot Noodle jumped straight on to my lap. 'Hello, boy,' I said, ruffling his head.

'ORSEY!' shrieked Bella, before climbing up on to the sofa and on to my lap too.

'Yes, ORSEY! Well done, Bella,' I said.

Bella looked me straight in the eye and then slapped me right across the face. **'OTTIE!'** she shrieked.

OMG – she can say my name! I mean, it might have been nicer if she hadn't slapped me but still – WOW!

'Yes, Bella, that's right! I'm Ottie!' I said, giving her a big cuddle.

Then Bella AND Pot Noodle jumped up and down on me, giving me tons of kisses and licks all over my face. It was pretty gross TBH, but it was also just what I needed after such an awful day.

ARGH, STOP! IT TICKLES!

TUESDAY 7 FEBRUARY

I'm avoiding everyone, or everyone is avoiding me. I don't even know any more.

I spent break time with Daniel, but he was playing footie at lunch, so I wandered towards the canteen, kind of hoping and dreading at the same time that I'd bump into the girls.

I saw Molly and Poppy sitting at a table by the windows. I didn't know whether I should go over or not, but I felt more confident seeing that Amber wasn't there.

'Hi,' I said quietly, sitting down.

'Hi,' they both said, smiling.

As they seemed happy to see me, I felt a bit less scared. 'Where are Jess and Amber?' I asked.

'At the library. Jess needed to return some books and

369

Amber went with her,' said Molly.

My heart sank knowing they were together, wondering if they were talking about me . . . wondering what they were saying . . .

We fell silent for a minute and then, before I could overthink it or stop myself, I said, 'I don't like not being friends.'

'Me neither,' said Molly, a smile breaking out on her face.

'Nor me,' agreed Poppy. 'I guess we feel sort of . . . stuck in the middle.'

'It's so silly. Why don't we try and work everything out?' continued Molly.

'I'd really like to,' I said sadly, 'but I'm not sure Amber wants to . . . I don't even know if Jess does.'

'They will. It's just a stupid misunderstanding,' reasoned Molly. 'We'll talk to them . . .'

'TQOEG are stronger than this!' said Poppy, putting

an arm round me.

I smiled at them gratefully. I really, really hope they are right.

PS I guess you won't be at all surprised to learn that every time I walked down the school corridors between lessons at least two people buzzed at me. I have gone right off bees now!

(6.11 p.m.)

I just found out something extraordinary.

I was eating a Penguin biscuit and then Mum goes, 'Did
you know that the inside of a Penguin is just a Bourbon
biscuit?'

I DID NOT KNOW THIS!!

I immediately picked up my phone to WhatsApp Jess
and then remembered I couldn't, as we weren't talking
any more. I tried to think of someone else who would
be really excited about it, but there wasn't anyone, and
it made me realize just how much I missed my BFF.

WEDNESDAY 8 FEBRUARY

Molly and Poppy were wrong; they were so completely wrong.

I kept my distance from the gang again today. I was hoping it would give Molly and Poppy a chance to talk to Amber and Jess about working everything out, but they obviously didn't bother, or maybe they did . . . but Amber and Jess didn't want to know.

Do you want to know how I know this?

I was looking through my Insta stories and I saw a photo of the whole gang . . . at Amber's house!

BESTIES

She'd also added this cute little animation saying BESTIES – it felt like I'd been stabbed in the heart. I mean, where was MY invite?!?!

It's clear now that TQOEG is well and truly over AND it's also 127 million gazillion per cent proof they have been making secret plans on their new WhatsApp group and **I'VE BEEN LEFT OUT!!!!**

(7.41 p.m.)

I can't stop looking at the photo. It's making me feel so sad. I know I've made mistakes, but I don't deserve to be ostrichsized, do I?

That's a strange word, isn't it? I wonder how it came about . . . I mean, are ostriches often left out of stuff? I hope not – as that's pretty mean. ☹

(7.46 p.m.)

I looked up the meaning and I realized I got the word wrong. It's 'OSTRACIZED' and it's actually got nothing to do with ostriches.

This is what it means: *To avoid someone on purpose, or to stop a person from taking part in the activities of a group.*

I'm glad that it's got nowt to do with poor ostriches, but I'm sad that it's **BANG ON** for what's happening to me.

7.53 p.m.

Saying that, I guess there is nothing to stop it happening to an ostrich, is there? I mean, it's a bit of a tongue twister, but you could be an ostracized ostrich!

7.59 p.m.

Imagine if the excluded ostrich's name was Ozzy? He could be Ozzy the Ostracized Ostrich – ha!

Quite a good name for a kids' picture book TBH, maybe I'll write it one day . . .

Argh – I'm getting distracted. What was I annoyed about again?!

Oh, yes – being ~~ostrichsized~~ ostracized!

8.45 p.m.

Asked Mum for advice as she's always good with stuff like this.

You see, a whole big part of me wanted to shout and scream and ask the gang why they've done this to me, but Mum convinced me it was better to calm down and sleep on it, because hopefully I'll be able to approach it more rationally in the morning. She also said that often it's better to talk face to face because text messages can be misconstrued (I had to look that up in the dictionary too, but what it means is that it's easy to get the tone of messages wrong and read them in a way that they weren't intended).

Then I asked Felicity for advice as she's sometimes good for stuff like this . . .

Is it true. . . . Do the gang really want me out?!

I'm feeling nice, so no – the gang is stronger than this!

PS. . . my name is still Brian!!

9.45 p.m.

I'm lying in bed, feeling anxious and worried about tomorrow. I found myself twiddling my necklace – the one that me and Jess bought each other a year ago.

I'll never take it off, no matter what happens, but I wonder if Jess is still wearing hers? I really hope so. I miss her so much x

THURSDAY 9 FEBRUARY

7.44 a.m.

Nervous, nervous, nervous and a little sprinkle of nervous on top. What a horrible-sounding sundae!

I'm so glad Coco the Monkey is back, because I really felt like I needed a sugar boost today.

Mum said to remain calm and rational and remember to listen, but I'm really not sure how I am even meant to start the conversation. I mean, what do I say? How do I ask them what they were doing? How do I react if they tell me what I'm most dreading? . . . That they don't want to be friends with me any more??

I can barely even begin to imagine how that would feel. I'd be devastated 😟

5.05 p.m.

So . . . if you were hoping for a dramatic scene, then you are in luck.

I'll get to it, but first take five minutes and make yourself a cup of hot chocolate (preferably with marshmallows and squirty cream) because we have A LOT to unpick.

OOOOPS! Hang on a sec. Maybe you're in bed and you've already brushed your teeth . . . in which case you'll have to make do with a glass of water. I've enough problems of my own and I don't want to get on the wrong side of your parents – or the tooth fairy, for that matter!!

Right, here we go . . .

When I got to school, Molly and Poppy said hi to me as normal; Amber and Jess were quiet but there was nothing new there. I decided it was probably best to wait until lunch to confront them, because there was more time and also because Daniel had agreed to come with me for moral support.

By the time me and Daniel got to the canteen, we could already see the girls sitting down and eating. I took a deep breath – it was either now or never!

I strode over to them, trying to look as confident as I could (even though my legs felt like jelly).

'Did you all have a nice time last night then?' I said.

Amber rolled her eyes and the rest of them looked quite confused.

'What do you mean?' asked Poppy.

'I mean at Amber's house? Because I saw it on your stories, you know,' I explained.

'Yeh, it was fun, but obviously it was a shame you couldn't come,' said Molly.

What was she talking about?

'Bit hard to come if you don't know anything about it,' I said.

'But Amber said you couldn't come . . .' said Poppy.

'Where was this?' I demanded. 'On your new secret WhatsApp group that I'm not allowed to join?'

Jess looked at Amber. 'You said that Lottie was seeing Daniel?'

Amber took a nail file out of her bag and began to file her nails. 'Oh, did I? Well, she usually is, so maybe I just assumed.'

I was feeling really cross now!

'You're lying, Amber! Are you ostrichsizing me on purpose?'

'What have ostriches got to do with this?' asked Poppy.

'Argh, I mean *ostracizing*,' I said. 'Amber, you keep making out that I'd prefer to be with Daniel than my friends, and it's NOT TRUE.'

'Isn't it?' said Jess sadly. 'That's what happened at the Bad Pancakes gig . . .'

'It isn't though, Jess. That's not what happened at all. Amber told me that you'd gone off with Cleo and that the others had gone to sit down. She said I should hang out with Daniel, then she made out that I couldn't wait to get rid of you.'

'What? Is that true, Amber?' said Jess.

'No, of course not,' said Amber.

'That's exactly what you said,' said Daniel. 'I was there too, remember!'

Amber let out a big sigh, as if she was totally bored of the conversation. 'God, this is dull. I mean, who cares anyway? The fact is you haven't been a very good friend to us lately – we *never* see you any more.'

'It's pretty hard when you keep purposely leaving me out!'

'I can't be bothered with this,' said Amber, standing up. 'Is anyone coming?'

No one moved.

'I said, *Is anyone coming?* Because, let's face it, I don't think me and *her* can be in the same gang any more, so you may as well choose which one of us you'd rather hang with.'

'What are you talking about, Amber?' asked Poppy.

'You can't seriously expect us to choose!' said Molly.

'That's exactly what I expect,' said Amber, putting her hands on her hips.

I felt sick. Was I about to lose all my best friends in one go?

'You can't make us do that, Amber,' said Jess. 'We're never going to let Lottie go.'

I looked up and met Jess's eyes. I'd never been more grateful to her in my life.

Without another word, Amber stormed off, leaving us all in complete shock.

TQOEG WhatsApp group:

> Amber has left the group.

> **ME:** WHAAAAAAAAAAAAAAAAAAAAAAAAAT!!!!

> **POPPY:** NOOOOOOOOOOOOOOOOOOOOOOOOOOOO!

> **MOLLY:** Is she serious?!?!

> **ME:** Oh gawd, sorry, guys. I feel like this is all my fault.

> **POPPY:** It's really not your fault, Lottie.

> **ME:** But she's had a tough time lately with her parents' divorce and that thing with Casper . . .

MOLLY: And we've all tried to be there for her, but she can't take it all out on you – it's not fair.

JESS: The girls are right, Lottie. I think she's looking for someone to blame and unfortunately it seems to be you.

POPPY: Hopefully she'll come round soon and apologize. We all know she likes a bit of drama.

ME: True dat

THOUGHT OF THE DAY:

I really don't know how to feel. I hate there being bad vibes between me and Amber, and I hate that she feels she had to leave the group. I really hope Poppy is right, because tomorrow is the last day of school before half-term, and I think we are all hoping that we can fix things before the holidays.

FRIDAY 10 FEBRUARY

5.05 p.m.

We didn't see Amber at break or lunchtime; she was clearly avoiding us. After school, we headed to Frydays and I was half hoping and half dreading seeing her there.

We ordered our chips and were having a good time laughing and joking and talking about our plans for half-term, when TUMGG walked in and the atmosphere immediately changed. The biggest shock was that there were three of them – at first, we didn't recognize their newest recruit (she looked different, with a TUMGG signature bun) but with horror we slowly realized . . .duh duh duh . . .

It was AMBER!!!

The whole gang inhaled deeply.

'Why's she with them?' whispered Poppy.

'I've no idea,' replied Molly. 'Weren't they the ones spreading rumours about her?!'

'Yeh . . . AND they were the ones making fun of me and Lottie,' said Jess.

'I don't think I like this,' I said nervously.

As they walked to the counter to order their food, they pushed past us, and Candice made a super-mean comment about me. She did it in a fake whisper, but it was obviously loud enough for us all to hear, and Izzy G and Amber burst out laughing.

'Hey, that's –' Jess began to say, clearly trying to stick up for me, but I pulled her back.

'Don't worry about it. Let's just ignore them,' I said.

Our food was ready before long and it was too cold to hang about, so we decided to walk home while eating our chips. Me and Jess said goodbye to Molly and Poppy (who were walking the opposite direction), and as soon as it was just the two of us, Jess turned to me and whispered, 'I have a confession to make.'

'Oh, yeh – what?' I asked.

'You know the bees project . . . well, you didn't research the wrong section. I looked at my notebook when I got home, and it was me that got it mixed up. So, I'm the one to blame for getting a U.'

'What?! Jess, I made a complete idiot out of myself – I can't go more than about five metres at school without someone doing a bee impression of me . . .'

'I'm really sorry, Lottie,' she said, clearly trying to hold in a laugh. 'But the good news is that I spoke to Miss

Dodson – I explained everything, and she agreed we can do it again after half-term.'

I wasn't sure if that was good news exactly, but I didn't say so. I was still in shock at Jess's revelation – she's ALWAYS on top of schoolwork.

'Are you absolutely a hundred per cent sure it was you?' I said. 'I mean, getting mixed up is a much more *me* thing to do . . .'

'I'm sure. I guess I've had a lot on my mind lately . . . Maybe everyone finding out that I'm gay has been a bit tougher on me than I've let on.'

I put my arm round her and gave her a big hug.

Remember I'm always here for you, Jess.

Thank you, Lotts.

Then for the first time in ages we got a chance to properly catch up. She told me that everything is cool between her and Cleo. Apparently she didn't even really have a crush on them, and it was Amber who was pushing her into it. Jess says she's really happy being single for now and I'm glad to hear that. Even though I'm happy with Daniel, I can't deny that relationships do make things kinda complicated!

'Listen, Jess,' I told her as we got to her house. 'I've made plans to see Daniel tomorrow, but I could cancel? I'd be great to hang out with you instead.'

'Nah, don't be silly, Lottie. I've got to help Mum with Florence tomorrow anyway. Daniel's your boyfriend and you should hang out with him too – I never minded about that.' Then she sighed. 'It sounds silly now, but Amber made me believe you were trying to ditch us, and I was worried I was going to lose you . . .'

I stopped and turned to face her, so I could look her straight in the eyes. 'I would never ditch you, NEVER!'

Jess grinned. 'Even if I decided to only ever walk like this,' she said, doing a pretty good impression of a penguin waddling.

'That would only make me like you more.'

'Even if I stopped showering and had BO that you could smell from five miles away?'

'I'd just wear a peg on my nose when I saw you.'

'Even if I wore a unicorn horn to school every day?'

I pointed at my earmuffs. 'Think about who you are talking to, Jess!'

She laughed. 'Even if I grew my fingernails super long like the ones you see in the Guinness World Records books and I couldn't even use my hands?'

I laughed. 'Even then, and I'd hold your bubble tea for ya.'

7.03 p.m.

OOH!

ME: I forgot to tell you something incredibly important today!!!!!!!!!!

JESS: Well, it was a pretty eventful day . . .

ME: I know but this is MEGA!

JESS: Come on then – don't leave me hanging.

ME: OK, prepare yourself . . .

ME: Did you know that the inside of a Penguin is just a Bourbon biscuit?

JESS: I DID NOT KNOW!!! 🤯

ME: I found that out this week and I immediately thought how much you'd love that fact!

JESS: I do love it! AMAZING!!

JESS: I just remembered I also wanted to ask you something today . . . Why were you going on about ostriches earlier??

ME: 🤣 🤣 🤣 I just like em!

JESS: As much as sloths and capybaras??? 😱

ME: Not quite, but I don't like the thought of them being left out – it's not their fault they're a bit weird!

JESS: Ain't that the truth!

ME: I never took my Weirdo 1 necklace off BTW . . .

JESS: I never took my Weirdo 2 necklace off either 🖤

THOUGHT OF THE DAY:
I cannot even begin to tell you how good it feels to have my BFF back. I truly believe that there is no one on earth quite like Jess – she really is one in a squillion.

SATURDAY 11 FEBRUARY

I feel like a weight has been lifted off my shoulders –
the sun is shining, the birds are cheeping, Dad is still
singing Bad Pancakes tunes (loudly and badly), Mum is
hoovering, Toby has farted on me twice already, Bella
is trying to feed toast to the DVD player, and Pot
Noodle is currently . . . **OH MY GOD, HE'S HUMPING
MY UNICORN SLIPPERS!!!**

Anyway, what I was getting at is that all is good (or at
least normal) in the Brooks household and I am just off
to have a nice relaxing bath before my date!

OMG, I've been invaded – twice!!

It is not possible to have any space, privacy or relaxation in this household!!

I just had the most dreamy day. I met Daniel at the

bus stop (he came to the one closest to my house) and
we got the bus into town. We sat upstairs at the back,
and he shared his earbuds with me and we listened to
some Bad Pancakes songs – I'm becoming a mega fan
now.

We got off the bus at Churchill Square. We had zero
plans, but instead of stressing about trying to decide,
we just wandered around, chatting and looking in shop
windows.

First, we went into Offspring, which is a cool trainer
shop on Duke Street – they do so many fun colour
combos that you'd never find in one of the big sports
shops. I remembered a game I used to play with Molly
where we'd choose each other outfits to wear in clothes
shops and never buy them (and the staff would get
really annoyed). I suggested to Daniel that we should
choose each other a pair of trainers and try them on.
He's obsessed with trainers, so he thought it was a
great game.

We agreed on a five-minute time limit. This is what we
came back with:

Me: Size five lime green, black and white Air Jordans.

Him: Size five bubblegum pink and white Superstars.

We both tried them on and were pretty pleased with each other's choices. He really liked his, but thought they were kind of bright to wear every day. I LOVED my bubblegum Superstars so much that I would have added them to my Christmas list or birthday list if I very annoyingly hadn't just had both of them. I couldn't get them for myself either as my bank balance was a disappointing £14.92.

'I can't wait to be an adult,' I said, 'and be able to buy myself trainers whenever I like.'

'Oh, really! And how are you going to make all your money?' asked Daniel with a cheeky smile.

'Simple, I'm going to be a famous author and cartoonist!'

'That'd be cool – did you ever watch an episode of *Cribs* on MTV where the movie stars have WHOLE rooms dedicated to trainers?'

'Ha ha, yeh, and huge garages, swimming pools, home cinemas and the biggest fridges you EVER saw.'

'What do they even put in those fridges anyway?!'

'More trainers probably,' I said, and Daniel laughed.

Sadly, I had to leave my bubblegum trainers behind, and we decided to wander off down the Lanes. I think we were both feeling a bit hungry, because when we were walking past Bond Street Coffee, Daniel suggested getting some banana bread, which is apparently the best he's ever tasted. He wasn't wrong – it was delicious! Daniel insisted on paying, so when I saw that Shakeaway was just next door I bought us milkshakes too: Kinder Bueno and KitKat Chunky for me, and Skittles and Marshmallow for Daniel. (I thought his sounded gross TBH, but it was way yummier than I thought!)

After that, we ended up in Snoopers Paradise, which is like an indoor jumble sale of vintage and boho stuff – retro toys, antiques, old books, sunglasses, costume jewellery, cool art prints and . . . I dunno just about everything you can think of. I've been going there since I was little, and you can get lost inside as it's huge.

We spent ages checking out the various stalls – the retro toys and games one is the coolest. It's mad how basic everything used to look, especially the gaming consoles with their massive cartridges. I also really liked a stall called Cute and Kitsch, which has all these funny little ceramic ornaments. I found one of a dog with a hole in its head. At first I was really confused, but then I realized it was a vase to put flowers in. I showed it to Daniel and he said it looked exactly like Pot Noodle! I really wanted to buy it, but I couldn't afford it. Hopefully it will still be there when I've saved up enough pocket money.

After we left, we were walking along Gardener Street and then Daniel stops suddenly and nudges me. 'Lottie, look – shall we?' He was pointing at the Photomatic shop.

Part of me was cringing, thinking of the shop assistant laughing at us, BUT it had been such a good day that I also thought it would be great to have some photos to remember it by. 'Why not?' I replied.

I needn't have worried after all. The shop assistant was a guy called Ben, and he was really nice. 'Been here before?' he asked. When we told him we hadn't, he explained how it worked (they have a colour and a black-and-white booth) and showed us all the props that we could use. I was excited and it turned out to be really fun.

Ben printed two copies of our photos, so we got a set each to take home. What do you think?

I love them so much. I'm going to hide them from my NOSY family though, as I know they'll laugh, especially at the last one!

SUNDAY 12 FEBRUARY

WHAT HAVE I GOT TO DO TO GET SOME PRIVACY AROUND HERE?!?!

My annoying little brother has been rifling through my stuff!! Apparently he was looking for a pair of scissors, and now he is running around the house, waving my photobooth pics around and shouting, 'Does anyone want to see something disgusting?'

Before I could get them off him, Mum said, 'Oooh, let's have a peek!' Then she and Dad looked at them and they saw the one of me and Daniel kissing and went 'OOOOOOOH!' and laughed, and now I want to DIE!

I grabbed a baguette from the kitchen counter and was about to batter him around the head with it, when Dad goes, 'Lottie, may I just remind you of your New Year's resolutions? In particular I'm talking about Number Eight!'

'DAMMIT,' I said, remembering what I'd written: *Be more tolerant of my very intolerable siblings.*

Well, there is only so far you can be pushed!

'Sorry, Dad . . . Sorry, Mum,' I said, before bringing the baguette down on Toby's head.

URGH! GROSS! It looks like a TONGUE KISS!

FYI – it was deffo NOT a tongue kiss. I've told you before, but I think tongue kissing is disgusting and I am never doing that in my life!

MONDAY 13 FEBRUARY

Woke up with a brilliant idea today!! First part of the plan involved messaging Daniel . . .

ME: I had a great day on Saturday!

DANIEL: Me too ♥

ME: You know it's a kind of a special day tomorrow . . .

DANIEL: Oh yeh – it's the anniversary of when you got together with Dan the Man!

ME: STOP

DANIEL: OK, OK, it's Valentine's Day – so I assume you have something super romantic planned for me???

ME: Errr, well, yeh, about that . . .

DANIEL: Hit me with it. I can take it 😬

ME: I don't want this to come across the wrong way, but I feel like I've not been the best friend in the world to Jess, Molly and Poppy lately – so I was thinking of maybe doing something with them tomorrow instead. Would you mind?

DANIEL: That's it – we're over! Have a nice life 🙁

ME: Really?!

DANIEL: Course not – I'm joking, you doughnut 🍩 That sounds cool, and I know the feeling – I think I've neglected Theo a bit lately too. Plus, we have football training and I'm not sure he and the lads would ever forgive me if I missed it for a romantic candlelit meal!

ME: 😜 True dat! Right, byeeeeee – I've got lots of organizing to do!!

DANIEL: Byeeeeee and good luck!

OK, I know what you are wondering . . . What has she got planned?!

Well, I'm afraid I'm too busy to tell you right now, so you'll just have to be patient, won't you? Because I've got to get to work!

TUESDAY 14 FEBRUARY

Happy Valentine's Day!!

Woke up early and came downstairs to find Dad
making heart-shaped pancakes in the kitchen, and
old-people romantic ballads were playing on the Sonos.

'Happy Valentine's Day, Lottie! Strawberry and cream
for you?'

'Thanks, Dad. Happy Valentine's Day,' I said, sitting
down at the table and pouring myself a glass of orange
juice.

There was a card propped up against the breakfast
cereal. At first, I thought maybe it was from Daniel, but
then I saw the French stamp – OMG, Antoine!

I felt a little nervous opening it. I really did not need
any more complications in my life.

Inside it read . . .

Mon petit dustbin,

Happy day of love!

I hope you are not as ridiculously sad as I assume you are. Your rejection of Antoine was a volcanic explosion of a mistake, and you must live with that. (It must be so sad ☹ boo hoo.)

Hopefully in time (maybe twenty-five to thirty-five years) your broken organs will begin to heal, and you will find a new 'bloke' (see, I am getting good of English) that is <u>almost</u> as good as me. But I hope it will not be Daniel the Brown Toilet Deposit, as he seemed similar to a soggy piece of cardboard.

Anyhoooo, enough about you, let us talk about <u>Antoine</u> . . .

My life is one long success – hurrah! Everything is easy for people who are exceptionally good-looking, which you will find it hard to understand. I have upgraded the girlfriend that was Amelie to a better one called Camille. She is similar but with smaller forehead and a less annoying voice.

Well, I have given enough of my time to you. I must go and balance a pineapple on my head.

Love, peace, cheese,

Antoine x

PS I hope your ears will be glad to know that my Gigantic Thumb Disease is now 78% curated.

I grinned to myself. It was lovely (and a bit weird) of him to send me a card. I'll send him a thank-you message later. More importantly, I had to text the girls!

TQOEG WhatsApp group:

ME: Happy Valentine's Day, babes!!!

JESS: Right back at ya xxxx

MOLLY: Have a super Valentine's, everybody!

POPPY: Happy V day! Love you all! xx

JESS: You got something romantic planned with Daniel, Lotts?

ME: No. I was hoping you guys might be free actually?

MOLLY: Us?! For what?!

ME: Well, come to my house for 7 p.m. and you'll find out . . .

POPPY: This all sounds very mysterious, Lottie. What are you up to?!

ME: Never mind that – can you come or not?!?!

MOLLY: Yes!!

POPPY: Deffo 😊 x

JESS: I'd love to! X

ME: YAY!

MOLLY: Are you going to ask Amber, Lotts?

ME: Yeh, I'll send her a message. I'm still hoping we can sort things out.

MOLLY: I've been a bit worried she might join TUMGG for good ☹

POPPY: Don't say that ☹

JESS: Let's stay positive – she'll come around, guys!

Step One of the Secret Valentine's Day Plan accomplished!

(6.33 p.m.)

PHEW – I'm exhausted!

The house is clean and tidy, and the family are all in uniform(!!)

Don't they scrub up well! *

* Apart from Bella who got kind of angry about the whole thing.

* Apart from Toby who keeps sticking his tongue out.

* Apart from the professor who ate his bow tie.

I have my hair curled and I'm wearing one of Mum's black evening dresses. It's fitted and sparkly and, even though it was a bit too big, she used a silver belt to nip it in at the waist. When I looked in the mirror after getting ready, I thought I looked good but also not quite myself, so I added the burger earmuffs and now I feel much more me.

I have one bit of sad news though. I messaged Amber but I didn't get a reply. I mean, I'm not surprised, and part of me is relieved that I won't have to stress about how she'll act, but I still feel sad about the whole situation IYSWIM.

I'm gonna try not to worry about it tonight though, because tonight is about having FUN!

Speaking of which I'd better shoot – the girls will be here very soon and I'm going to triple-check the table decorations.

9.25 p.m.

OMG – that was so much fun!! I think the girls had a brilliant time too.

When they arrived, I was so pleased to see that they were all dressed up too, in their own unique way. Molly, as always, looked like a supermodel, standing tall in a short turquoise dress and gold sandals that went brilliantly with her long red hair. Jess was wearing an amazing neon-pink suit, which she'd found in a charity shop! And Poppy was wearing a baby-blue skater dress, and her hair was in a high pony.

'Good evening, ladies,' said Dad (who was dressed in a white shirt, black bow tie and black trousers). 'Let me take you through to the drinks reception.'

Jess giggled. 'The drinks reception?'

'This is all very posh, Lottie,' said Molly, looking excited.

'Yes, I feel like a proper lady,' said Poppy. 'In fact, I think you should all call me Lady Poppy tonight.'

'Of course,' I said, smiling. 'However, I think it should be pronounced "laaaaaaaady"!'

Poppy laughed. 'OK, Laaaaaaaady Lottie.'

We all followed Dad through to the living room, where there was classical music playing on the Sonos, like you'd have in a fancy wine bar.

Mum was waiting in there for us. She was dressed in a white shirt like Dad and a black skirt. She also had a tea towel over her arm and was holding out a bottle of champagne (*pssst*, it was really Appletiser – yummy). 'Would you like some bubbles, laaaaaaadies?' she asked.

'Yes, please,' we all said in unison.

She poured us each a drink in proper champagne flutes, and it all felt super mature.

'Would you care for the hors d'oeuvres now too?' she asked.

'*Horse-durfs?*' said Poppy.

'It's *hors d'oeuvres*,' I said, copying how Mum had said it. 'It's French.'

'What does it mean?' asked Jess. 'It's not snails, is it??'

TBH I didn't know what it meant. Considering that I had a French ex-boyfriend, you'd have thought I'd be a bit better at French by now!

Mum laughed. 'It's not snails. It means appetizers or finger food.'

'Or, in this case,' I said with a grin, as Toby appeared with a plate piled high with yellow puffs of deliciousness . . .

Everyone cheered and then I handed out the menus for the rest of my fancy dinner party – featuring all my faves!!

Lottie's Galentine's Day Dinner Party
14th February

Hors d'oeuvres
Monster Munch
(Pickled Onion and Flaming Hot)

Starter
Breaded chicken pieces
(AKA nuggets)

Main Course
Pot Noodle
(Chicken and Mushroom or Bombay Bad Boy)

Dessert
Vanilla ice cream
(with crushed KitKat Chunky)

All served with a choice of
red or white 'wine'

After the hors d'oeuvres had been obliterated (which took about five minutes), Dad came back into the room and announced, 'Your table is now ready for you, laaaaaaadies.'

We started to follow him to the dining room, and I was so excited for the girls to see what we'd done as I'd worked so hard (with help from my family) to make it like a classy restaurant. We had laid the table with a white tablecloth and a million different knives, forks and spoons, everyone had napkins folded all fancy like a fan, and I'd written name cards for each guest in gold ink. The ceiling spotlights were turned down low, and there were candles dotted around the room to make it extra atmospheric – **EEK**.

But I knew something was wrong when I heard Dad shout, **'NOOOOOOOO!'** and then a much ruder word (that I won't repeat here) that you would NOT usually hear in a fine dining establishment.

I pushed past the girls, and this is what I was greeted with . . .

Bella and Pot Noodle had somehow mountaineered up on to the table and were busy eating the chicken nuggets/smashing everything up. I dropped to my knees, absolutely devastated. All that hard work and preparation, and it had been ruined!

But then I heard the girls start to giggle as they took in the scene.

'Oh, Lottie!' said Molly. 'This is exactly the type of disaster that could only happen to you!'

I looked up to see Mum rescuing Bella (still shouting 'BUM!'), Dad shooing Pot Noodle off the table and grabbing the broom, and Toby stuffing the discarded nuggets into his gob as quickly as possible. Molly was right: it was chaos, but it was my chaos and I had to admit that it was kind of funny.

'I suppose there is one bit of good news,' I said. 'We still have Pot Noodles to eat!'

Poppy gasped and looked horrified.

'The instant noodles – not my dog!!' I said, laughing.

'Phew!!' she said, pretending to faint.

We ended up having two each (!) and what with all the ice cream and KitKats we felt truly stuffed. But it was so much fun, and I don't think I've laughed that much for ages.

At the end of the meal, Jess stood up and said, 'I'd like to make a toast to the Best Galentine's Day ever!'

We all raised our glasses of red wine (*pssst*, it was actually Ribena) and clinked them together.

It couldn't have gone any better, and I think the whole gang really appreciated it.

I couldn't help but feel a little sad, though, that our gang of five was now only a gang of four.

9.42 p.m.

Mum poked her head into my room, as I was getting ready for bed. 'Lottie, Daniel's at the door!'

What on earth was he doing here at this time?!

'I know it's late, but he says he just wanted to drop a present off for you, so I said it was OK.'

'Muuuuuuuum!' I hissed. 'You should have asked me first – I'm wearing my Little Mermaid pyjamas.'

'Oooh, surprised they still fit you, love!'

'They don't fit me! They are aged 7–8, but they're the only ones I have clean as no one ever does any washing around here!'

'Learn how to use the washing machine yourself and all your problems will be solved,' she smirked.

Argh, I hate it when she's so logical.

I put my dressing gown on and ran downstairs. Even though I was tired and a little bit annoyed he'd turned up unannounced, I couldn't help but smile when I saw his face.

'Happy Valentine's Day,' he said. 'Sorry to come by so late, but I didn't want to interrupt your party. I, errr . . . I got you a present and I wanted to give it to you today.' That's when I noticed he was hiding something behind his back.

'Thanks,' I said, trying to peek behind him. 'Are you going to give it to me then??'

He shuffled from one foot to the other – he was clearly quite nervous! Then he revealed what he was hiding and I think I did the biggest grin of my life!

It was the ceramic cockapoo vase that I'd seen in Cute and Kitsch on Saturday – the one I wanted to buy even though I didn't have any money left. AND he'd filled it with flowers!

'I can't believe you went back and got it!' I said.

'I can't believe you still wear Little Mermaid pyjamas,' he said, laughing.

Ooops – my dressing-gown belt had come undone. I punched him playfully on the arm.

'Happy Valentine's Day, Lottie,' he said.

'Happy Valentine's Day, Daniel.'

Then I looked behind me to check the hallway was Fun-Police-free and I kissed him.

FYI... I personally think it was at least 37.84% better than last time.

WEDNESDAY 15 FEBRUARY

I cannot seriously be on my last page already, can I?!
Sometimes I shock myself at how much I can ramble
on and on and on and on and on and on . . . I hope you
don't get bored!!

Today I feel half happy and half sad. I'm happy that
things are good with Daniel and that I've made up with
the gang, but I think you know what I'm feeling really
sad about, don't ya?

Yeh, it's all the stuff that's happened with Amber.

I know she's been tricky and, if I'm honest, quite
unkind, but I wish she would have let us help her. I
always assumed that she'd just apologize and we'd
move on. But seeing her on Friday made it clear that
wasn't going to happen . . . Now I'm kind of worried
she might join TUMGG and we'll never be friends
again, but I really hope not. Keep your fingers crossed
for TQOEG, please!

Right I need to dash. I can smell Dad making waffles

– so, without further delay, here comes part six (!!) of Lottie's Worldly Wisdoms . . .

Dear Lottie,

It's been an eventful year so far . . .

Yep, you can say that again, Lottie!

IT'S BEEN AN EVENTFUL YEAR SO FAR, LOTTIE!

OMG, why am I having a conversation with myself?!

Because that's the kind of weird stuff we do, Lottie . . .

OK, whatever, let's get on with it then.

Soooooo, what shall we say about the last few hundred pages? It's been a learning journey, for sure — hit me with those life lessons:

* Appreciate your family. Yes, they are annoying, embarrassing, smelly and odd, but that includes you too! And they love you, you know. They really truly do, and not everyone is as lucky as you to have that kind of love around them.

* It may be very exciting having a new boyfriend, BUT you should never neglect your friends — TQOEG 4EVA, remember!

* Stay away from your eyebrows.

* Dogs are smelly, disgusting, tiring, destructive and crazy — but they are also the best pets ever!!!!!! I love ya, Pot Noodle x

* Except for hamsters, obvs.

* Life is too short for silly, unachievable resolutions that you will NEVER keep. So, do you know what I say?

* Eat the KitKats!

* Wear the childish earmuffs!

* Hug your family!

* Be weird and blummin' own it!

Love Lottie ♥
xxx

PS Get a fortune-telling fish. They give the most ex-cellent advice! I really don't know what I would have done without Felicity ☺

Do you need more Lottie, more LOLs and more BFF Dramas in your life? If so, turn the page for a sneak peek of . . .

THE MEGA-COMPLICATED CRUSHES OF LOTTIE BROOKS

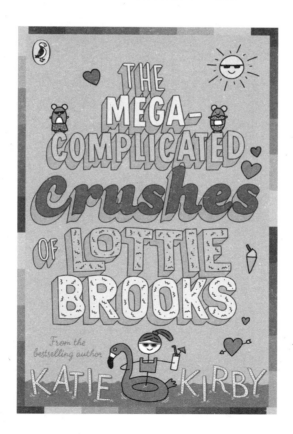

TUESDAY 3 MAY

7.12 a.m.

OMG OMG OMG!!!!!

Today I have to see Wotsit Fingers and maybe even speak to him . . .

I know we chatted last night but that was just on WhatsApp. Today it will be **IN PERSON,** which is completely different because it involves ACTUALLY seeing him with ACTUAL eyes and ACTUALLY speaking to him with ACTUAL lips.

OMG!!

I REALLY don't want to go all BRINE-DOOPEY again and mess it up because it's been going so well . . . In case you've forgotten, we have an ACTUAL date.

OMG!!!!!!!!!

Anyway, I'd better stop obsessing over Daniel and get dressed and do my teeth or I'll be late for school. I will update you ASAP when I get home.

Wish me luck!

Note to self: you really must stop saying OMG so much.

OK, I'm back.

So . . . as I was pretty late for school for reasons beyond my control, I didn't see Daniel at all until lunchtime.

There I was, standing in the lunch line with Jess, and he comes in with some mates.

Jess starts
nudging me
and going . . .

She clearly thought she was being really funny, when actually it was not very funny **AT ALL**. If I'd have been able to get a gag on her without drawing EVEN more attention to the situation, I would have, but instead I just gave her my best Death Stare.

I've been working on my Death Stare for about three and half years now. If you are interested in perfecting your own, here are my simple instructions:

How to perform the perfect Death Stare:

1. Open eyes really wide.

2. Tilt head slightly to the left.

3. Grit teeth while simultaneously pursing your lips.

4. Frown in a quizzical type of way that implies: **'WHAT ON EARTH DO YOU THINK YOU ARE DOING?!?!'**

I mean, I'll admit it's not exactly the most attractive look, but it gets the job done and that's what it's all about.

Anyway . . . sorry. Back to the story . . .

Suddenly Daniel is right there in front of me, and he gives me a really strange look.

That's when I remembered I was still doing my Death Stare – so I reorganized my facial features back into their usual positions.

Apart from the initial weirdness, you'll be really pleased to know that the convo went pretty well. I've written a transcript here as I know you must be **EXTRA MEGA INTERESTED** . . .

ME: Hey, Daniel!
DANIEL: Hey, Lottie.
ME: What are you having for lunch today?
DANIEL: I brought a cheese roll in. You?
ME: I'm getting a cheese panini.
DANIEL: Nice.
ME: Have you got crisps?
DANIEL: Yeh, Wotsits.
ME: Cool.

Five seconds of awkward silence

ME: Do you like Wotsits then?
DANIEL: Yeh.
ME: I thought you might . . . I just noticed that

	you eat them quite a lot . . . How often do you usually have them?
DANIEL:	Errr . . . not sure, maybe twice a week . . . Why? Are you monitoring my crisps consumption, Lottie?
ME:	NO! That would be weird . . .
DANIEL:	Yes, it would.
ME:	I just always find with Wotsits that the cheese powder can get a bit messy and sometimes it can get stuck under your fingernails, so you have to wash your hands extra super well afterwards . . . Do you find that too?
DANIEL:	Um . . . Maybe . . . I've not really noticed.
ME:	Hmmm.

Three more seconds of awkward silence

ME AND DANIEL AT THE SAME TIME: So . . .

Nervous laughter

DANIEL:	You still cool for next Saturday, yeh? Boho Gelato at 3?

ME: Yeh, great. See ya there!

I mean, it wasn't without fault. The cheese-powder part was maybe a *bit* intense, and I *may* have come across as a crisp-obsessed freak, BUT I did plant the seed about the potential cheese-powder-fingernail issue, so at least he's aware of the dangers now.

The most positive part was that all my words were **REAL ENGLISH WORDS** so I'm going to give myself an A+ for effort. Well done me.

The Being Able to
Speak Actual words
Award is presented to
        Lottie Brooks

THOUGHT OF THE DAY:
Must try and think of some conversation topics that don't revolve around crisps.

KATIE KIRBY is a writer and illustrator who lives by the sea in Hove with her husband, two sons and dog, Sasha.

She has a degree in advertising and marketing, and after spending several years working in London media agencies, which basically involved hanging out in fancy restaurants and pretending to know what she was talking about, she had some children and decided to start a blog called 'Hurrah for Gin' about the gross injustice of it all.

Many people said her sense of humour was silly and immature, so she then started writing the Lottie Brooks series.

Katie likes gin, rabbits, overthinking things, the smell of launderettes and Monster Munch. She does not like losing at board games or writing about herself in the third person.

EVERYONE
IS READING ABOUT LOTTIE'S EMBARRASSING LIFE. TOTAL NIGHTMARE!

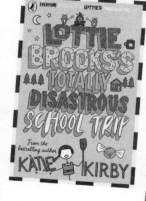